# SANCTIFIED

THE SAGA OF THE NANO TEMPLAR BOOK TWO

## JON DEL ARROZ

SILVER EMPIRE

# ONE

Kneeling at one of the *Justicar's* hard sanctuary pews had to be one of the most uncomfortable experiences in Drin's life. He'd stayed in this position for close to an hour while Father Cline and the elders debated what to do with him.

"Meditate in prayer," Cline had told him. He'd done so, and his knees ached from his humble position on the wooden kneeler.

Footsteps sounded from the back of the sanctuary. Cline arrived, dressed in formal white robes that accentuated his green Elorian skin. He stopped in front of Drin.

Drin did not look up.

"Arise, my son," Father Cline said.

Drin stood. Only then did he look Father Cline in the eyes. "Forgive me, Father, for I have sinned."

"You are forgiven, but penance is required. The elders have conferred." Father Cline paced in front of him, hands folded together, the sleeves of his robes draping over his knuckles. "Normally, a desertion would lead to excommunication, and the harsh removal of your nanites from your system."

Drin winced at the thought. He'd been prepared for it. He didn't dare pray for any other outcome. Whatever God's will would be was what would be done. He hoped the Lord conferred favor upon him for his other noble deeds.

"But," Father Cline said, unfolding his hands and raising a finger in the air, "one would have to be a blind man not to see the fruits of your good labor on Konsin II. The Sekarans had the Skree people enslaved, and thanks to your efforts in freeing them, they are now Yezuah's people. We have concluded it must have been God's will for you to come here, no matter the circumstances."

*That is what I've been trying to tell the elders since the* Justicar *arrived,* Drin thought. But he did not speak. It was not his place in this sanctuary.

"The lesson you must learn, when you have misgivings or are not certain of God's path for you, is to speak with your brethren and with me. I am here to guide you, my son, and I am always here to listen."

"Thank you, Father," Drin said.

"But we must maintain order among the Templars, nonetheless. I mentioned there would be penance," Father Cline said.

"Whatever penance you would have me assume is a mercy, Father."

"While aboard this ship and not attending to your regular duties as a Templar, you will act as a vassal. Your station will be beneath the other Templars, and your duties will include cleaning the latrines, preparing meals, and other ship maintenance duties normally be beneath your station. This penance is meant to teach you humility, and to rely on the others of this Holy Church."

Not too harsh a penalty. Drin had never been averse to work. He enjoyed keeping busy so he could keep himself from fretting over the violence of the battles he engaged in as a Templar. Even after liberating the city of Altequine from the Sekarans, Drin found himself abhorring violence. Sometimes it was necessary, but the faces of the enemies he'd slain in the name of the Lord still haunted him. "Thank you, Father," Drin said.

Father Cline stepped to the pew and placed both hands on Drin's shoulders. He bowed his head. Drin did the same. "Lord Yezuah on high, absolve Templar Drin of his sins. Make him a clean slate and an offering to you and your glory so he may always do your will and never stray. Bless us and bless all of your holy servants, may we dwell in your kingdom forever and ever, amen," Father Cline said.

"Amen," said Drin, lifting his head again.

Father Cline patted Drin's arms, then stepped back. "Now that the unpleasantries are over, let's get to business. You still have your duties as a Templar we must prioritize above your penance. You're one of the best warriors and leaders we have, Drin, and I'm much relieved the elders didn't vote to strip you of your nanites and your power."

"I am, as well," Drin said.

"As you may be aware, Altequine is not the only city on Konsin II. It was a miracle that you led these slaves in a revolt and got as far as you did without Church support, but now we are here, and we should do all we can to ensure the rest of this planet is free from Sekaran heresy and abuse."

"My sword is ever ready to do glory to Yezuah's name," Drin said.

"Of that, I have no doubt. Our reconnaissance teams show the city of Shiraz is the next largest Sekaran stronghold on this planet, which is across the desert, into the mountains in the east. You will join your former unit in an assault there to remove the warlord tyrant and bring the gospel to the people of Shiraz."

"I am honored to serve," Drin said, bowing his head.

Father Cline moved to the altar, where he had a bowl of

blessed water. He dipped his fingers in it and returned to Drin, sprinkling it on Drin's forehead. "Now, go and be with your brethren. They've been diminished without you."

Drin mouthed a prayer, keeping his hands folded and his head bowed low as he left the sanctuary. At the back of the rustic-themed room, automatic doors opened into the metallic hallways of the Elorian warship. Drin turned to head to the recreation room, where the other Templars would be gathered.

He arrived to see his full unit there. They cheered for him and greeted him with hugs and slaps on the back. It was like he'd never left in the first place.

"Drin!" Jellal said. Slightly taller though less muscular than Drin, Jellal had been the Templar Drin considered his closest friend. "It's good to see you again, brother."

"You as well," Drin said.

Baifed, another Templar, with long hair tied back like the warriors of old, clasped him on the arm. "I'm pleased to find you're alive and not a traitor to the cause."

"Did you really convert a whole city on your own, and without a copy of the Holy Book to reference?" Jellal asked.

"I was never alone. The Lord was with me from the beginning. And I had help."

"The Pyus girl, with the ears, yeah?" Jellal asked, pointing fingers up over his head to mimic the long, floppy-eared Pyus features.

"I've heard disconcerting rumors that she has the nanites coursing through her veins," Baifed said. The scowl on his face dampened the jovial mood of all of the other Templars in the room, more than a dozen in all.

"The rumors are true," Drin said. Women traditionally weren't allowed nanites, as the original apostles of Yezuah had all been male. Drin had been reluctant to allow Anais, the Pyus girl, to take the nanites from his bloodstream and bond with her, but if he hadn't, she would have died.

"Heresy," Baifed said under his breath.

"Unorthodox, not heresy. At least, until the elders decide what to do with her," Jellal said.

"She fought valiantly," Drin said, his tone coming out more defensive than he would have liked. "Without her, I would have not been able to take Altequine and complete the conversion of its residents. She is eager to help and has a kind soul, much like Marayh, one of Yezuah's first followers. You recall her story, yes?"

Baifed looked none too impressed. "Quizzing me on the Holy Book will not change matters. It's disgraceful for her to have nanites, regardless the circumstance."

From the back of the room, two hands clapped loudly together. Drin looked over to see the commander of his unit, Shayne. "Let's leave the theological debates until later and celebrate the fact brother Drin is back among us, shall we?" Shayne said.

He came over to Drin, and the two men shook hands. "Commander," Drin said. It was comforting to see Shayne again. These past months, Drin had to assume leadership on his own, something he had never wanted to do, even if the Lord called him to the task.

"We're glad to have you back," Shayne said.

"And glad we'll get to fight by your side again," Jellal said.

"You still remember the unit formations? Or should we hold you in reserves for this next battle?" Shayne asked. A twinkle in his eye let Drin know he was teasing.

"I'd like to see someone try to hold me back from this battle," Drin said, grinning. "The Sekarans of this world still have much to answer for."

Shayne nodded. "Then enjoy this evening and be merry. Tomorrow at dawn, we will bring the wrath of God to the Sekarans. They will repent, or they will perish!"

The Templars in the room cheered, and Drin spent the rest of the evening catching up with old friends. After all of his doubt about his path, he found he missed his old life. It was much easier not to have to be the one giving the orders. In this coming battle, he would be content to follow.

# TWO

Anais spent yet another day strapped to a table, poked and prodded with needles, with more than a dozen wires attached to her fur, monitoring her vitals. Elorians hovered around her, but, thankfully, her friend, Lyssa, was allowed to sit with her. It was nice just to have another Pyus present. It brought her a small sense of home through an uncomfortable situation.

"What do you think they're trying to do with you? Are you some sort of experiment case?" Lyssa asked, keeping her voice quiet.

"I don't know," Anais said. "I never asked for their stupid nanites. Apparently, women never receive them. I'm getting tired of being looked at like I'm some abomination."

"I bet," Lyssa said. "And every day you're stuck in here is another day we can't return home."

Home. To Pyus. The thought made Anais frown. Sekarans kidnapped her from her planet, and she'd still not had a chance to contact her family. The night they took her was still a hazy blur in her mind. The Sekarans had moved so quickly. They made it sound like they'd murdered everyone at her estate, but she had no way to be sure. Once she escaped, she'd had no means to communicate off-world, and since they'd led a revolt among the Skree slaves, their king didn't want to send any interstellar transmissions, lest Sekarans intercept the message and realize something had gone very wrong on the planet.

She'd hoped the presence of the Elorians would change matters, but ever since they learned she had the nanites inside her, they'd kept her confined and treated her like a science experiment.

A woman entered the room, an older Elorian with drooping cheeks and a frumpy form, wearing a black habit as was custom among the nuns of the Elorian warship. Anais recognized her as Vith, one of the few Elorians who treated her with kindness.

"I have good news," Vith said, making her way to Anais's cot and tapping several buttons on the medical equipment. "We've run every test we can think of. Our data analysts will have information for years' worth of study, thanks to you. You're not only the first woman to have the nanites in generations, but you're the first non-Elorian in recorded history, as well. We very much appreciate you willingly submitting yourself to our medical testing, even if some of the others don't voice it to you."

"That is good news," Anais said. It drained her, lying here under constant surveillance. "First woman in generations? I was under the impression I was the first, period."

Vith unplugged some of the monitors and carefully detached them from Anais's fur. Then, she removed an IV. "Such matters are left out of the general studies history books, but there is ample evidence to suggest one of Yezuah's original followers, Marayh, had nanites bestowed upon her. Not many know about this, but in the Year of our Lord Three Hundred, there was a secret order of nuns called The Life's Breath of Eloria. They were said to do miraculous healings like only the apostles or the Templars could do. It's widely believed the women of that order had the nanites."

"What happened to them?"

"A Sekaran super-weapon blew up the planet where they were stationed," Vith said.

"Oh," Anais said. This war had so much bloodshed. It was amazing Pyus had managed to stay out of the fray for so long. But as a world controlled by commerce, they did their best to stay out of the conflict. Neutrality couldn't last forever, apparently.

"But the important part is, you're not alone. Perhaps women have different gifts than men, but we can all find our place in the Lord's divine plan, yes?" Vith smiled.

Anais nodded, but she wasn't as sure as this woman in her faith. It comforted her to learn other women had to deal with the nanites. With the way she'd been treated until this point by the Elorians, Anais had never felt more alone. The nanites separated her from everyone. Even Lyssa trod carefully around her because of those millions of tiny weapons inside of her.

One of the Templars entered her hospital room. Anais recognized him as Baifed. He was as large as Drin, with an even more stoic face, if such a countenance could be possible. He had a cleft chin, which made him easier to distinguish than some of the other Elorian men.

"The tests are done?" Baifed asked. His voice had a commanding sense to it, someone used to getting what he wanted.

"I don't believe there's any more information we need to obtain from her," Vith said. She disconnected some of the monitors. "She's all yours."

"All...his?" Anais asked. She hadn't been aware the Elorians intended on *giving* her to someone. It made her fur stand on edge and her tail tense behind her. Her long ears went erect. These were all defense mechanisms evolved on her world, but they came as naturally as any other instinct. She wanted to flee, but there was nowhere to go.

"For training," Baifed said. "I'm going to attempt to teach you enough control of your nanites so you won't be a danger to others around you. Dress and come with me," he said. He turned for the door and stepped outside.

Those sounded like orders, not a request. Anais clenched her teeth. She didn't like being told what to do. But she needed the help of these Elorians if she were going to keep herself safe.

Lyssa glanced at her worriedly. "Will you be okay?"

"I think so," Anais, said, sliding off the hospital bed. With the man gone, she removed her gown and put on her normal civilian clothes. She wore white to match her fur coloration, though the design of her clothes she'd gotten on the Sekaran-controlled world were far too modest for her tastes. She smoothed down her long skirt and exited the room. If nothing else, it would be good to be out of the hospital room.

Baifed motioned for her to follow him before striding down the long hallway. Anais kept pace with him.

"Nanites react to will. The stronger the will, the better the control. The first thing we learn when the Holy Church trains us is not to be wishy-washy about our desires. Most people are. Whether it's from embarrassment or lack of confidence, I don't understand it. But we had it trained out of us as children. We are one with the nanites, just as the nanites are one with our Lord."

The advice sounded esoteric to Anais. She didn't know how to apply what he said, but she stayed quiet. Anything he suggested to help her had to be better than what she currently understood about her powers. The nanites coursed through her veins, and she couldn't even feel them there. Did she need to have more faith that they would perform according to her will?

"The best way to be confident in your actions is to pray ahead of time. Ask God what His will is for you, and if you do so, you will change your path to align with His. Doing so makes the inter-action with the nanites much easier. "You *do* believe in the Lord Yezuah, yes?

Drin had wanted her to convert as part of their freeing of the

Skree slaves in Altequine. Anais had agreed she would, and she kept her word. Maybe there was a God out there like the Elorians said. She couldn't be sure, but she figured it would be better to gamble on appeasing such a God than ignoring His will if He were real. "I guess so," she said.

Baifed stopped in his walking for a moment to scrutinize her. "Good," he finally said, starting his walk again. They made their way into another wing of the hospital. There, he stopped again, in front of a room where a Skree sat.

"Vith believes the best way to maximize your powers will be to concentrate on healing. So, this is what we will do. Some of the Templars are excellent at healing, but most are not. I only have a mild skill with the nanites in this regard. But the principles of how to use the nanites are the same regardless of whether they're being used for healing or used for battle. Most Templars have a cursory amount of healing skill in order to accelerate the repair of damage we take in battle. Let's see if you'll be able to extend this to others."

They both moved toward the Skree, introduced themselves, and learned of the Skree's problems. He suffered burn wounds in a recent battle with the Sekarans, the worst of the charred flesh snaking up his arm and around his shoulder. When he pulled his sleeves up from the ground, he revealed an even more horrific wound. The burns were deep. He was lucky to be alive.

"It's from their laser-repeaters," the Skree said. "It stings, but I'm becoming used to it."

Anais stared at the wound. What could she do about it? She had helped Drin once, but their lives had been on the line. Her adrenaline had carried her more than any skill.

"You'll need to lay hands on the wound to begin," Baifed said.

"Won't it hurt?" Anais asked.

"Likely."

She took a deep breath and did as he said. She pressed both her hands against the Skree's burn wound. The skin felt rough, sticky, disgusting. She tried to choke down some of the bile rising in her throat. How did doctors do this on a regular basis? Did they desensitize themselves to such sensations?

"Now breathe," Baifed said. "In slowly, and out again. Relax. If you are tense it makes it harder for your nanites to clearly react to your will."

Anais took a breath through her nose and then out again. She could do this. She had to do this. These nanites would be bonded to her for her whole life. She had to utilize them.

"Now focus. The wound. Let it fill your mind and focus on the result you want. The nanites will repair the damage if they understand.

The Skree watched and waited. He didn't comment but appeared hopeful. These people had such faith in the Elorians after the Templars had liberated Altequine from the Sekarans. She wished she had such strong faith. But she focused her attention on the wound. It had to go away. The Skree needed to be restored. She pictured his dark skin tone as it would naturally be without the wound. The nanites would do the rest. A tingling sensation shot up her spine. Excited, she pulled her hands back.

The wound remained unchanged, but the Skree's face had tightened in pain.

Baifed frowned. "It's like working with a child," he said. He pressed his hands to the Skree's wounds. The Skree yelped from the rough handling. A small glow radiated from the Templar's fingertips. When Baifed pulled his hands back, however, the wound disappeared.

"How?" Anais asked. Why couldn't she have done what he did? From what she could tell, her efforts had been useless.

"You don't have faith," Baifed said. He frowned. He shook his head. "I knew it was wrong for a woman to carry the nanites. Father Cline should purge these from you."

"That's an option?" Anais asked. Maybe it would be best to get the machines out of her body.

"Sometimes. The procedure is *very* painful, and it results in death more often than not."

Anais gasped. "You want me dead?"

"It's not what I want. If the Lord wills it, then it is the Lord's prerogative. I can't help but feel it is an insult to Him to have the nanites running through your body. Both as an outsider and as a woman. It's a mockery of the faith."

*Tell me how you really feel*, Anais thought. She could hardly believe he advocated for her death rather than wishing for her to continue with the nanites. Tears welled in her eyes, but she swore she wouldn't cry. She hated these people. The Elorians were all so stuffy. Except Drin. Well, even Drin could be very stuffy, if she were honest with herself. But at least he had some sense to him. She wanted off her planet and wished she could be back on Pyus. "I want to talk to whoever is in charge," she said. "I want to return to my people."

Baifed dismissed the Skree, who seemed content to extricate himself from the situation, hustling out the door. Baifed then looked at Anais. "We'll have to talk to Father Cline about that, as well. But it would be sensible for you to go back to your world rather than live among us a stranger."

"Yeah," Anais said. Thinking about her homeland tugged on her heart. She hoped everyone was alive, at the very least, though she had the feeling she shouldn't count on it. There had to be a way to contact them. "Then let's go visit Father Cline."

Baifed mad a sour expression. "You mean request an audience with him."

"Whatever," Anais, said. "Just take me to him. Would you?"

Baifed looked at her as if he wanted to flat refuse but, instead, he motioned for her to follow. "I'll lead you to him, but I warn you, if you treat him as you treat me, you'll find yourself wishing you'd displayed more respect."

More respect. Anais hadn't said anything wrong. But she clamped her jaw shut anyway. There was no sense in arguing, especially when she wanted something from the Elorians, and Baifed just wanted to fight.

She had to find a way to get to her home planet.

Baifed grunted and led her through the ship, *The Justicar*, as several people had called it. The corridors were plain, save for a symbol representing a table paced every few feet along the wall, which represented Yezuah's bringing together of the twelve tribes of Eloria. The markings made the ship look ancient, though, in reality, it probably had more modern technology than anything her people could muster on Pyus.

They entered a large chamber with several wooden pews in between backlit stained-glass on either side of the room. Ahead of them was a dais with a table and a long cloth outstretched, along with three candles providing flickering light. An Elorian knelt at the table, muttering a prayer. He had white hair, in a crown-shape along his otherwise bald head, and didn't appear to see them enter. Since he was the only person there, Anais presumed he was Father Cline.

Baifed made his way up between the pews to the center of the room and knelt behind the man. Anais followed to the pew. When Baifed looked at her expectantly, she decided to kneel with him.

Father Cline spent several more moments in prayer before he stood and turned around. He didn't appear surprised to see them. "Rise, my children," he said. His voice was low and soothing, with the slightest of rasps to it.

"Thank you for speaking with us, Father. Glory to Yezuah," Baifed said.

"Glory to Yezuah," Father Cline said.

Anais remained silent. She couldn't be sure what would upset the Elorians. It seemed better to remain quiet than to say something out of place.

"The outsider wished to request an audience," Baifed said. He took a breath as if he were going to continue speaking, but Father Cline lifted his hand. Baifed shut his mouth.

"The Lord has bestowed her with the nanites. We cannot refer to her as an outsider any longer. She is our sister."

Baifed's lips tightened, but he nodded.

Father Cline turned his attention to Anais. "Now what is it, my child? How might I help you?"

"I want to go home," Anais said. The words came out more childish than she would have liked to have sounded. Her voice was high, almost like a squeak. But it was her true sentiment. She missed Pyus and her family. It was hard to resist the tears welling in her eyes, but she did her best. "My planet is Pyus. My people are there. The Sekarans invaded and...I'm not sure if they're alive. I need to find out."

Father Cline's gaze lingered on her as if he peered into her soul. "I see," he finally said. "I don't believe it would be prudent to dispatch you to a planet controlled by the blasphemers. You would likely be captured or killed."

"Couldn't you send some of the Templars with me? I've seen what just one can do here," Anais said.

"We are not your personal army," Baifed muttered.

Father Cline held up a hand. "My child, to deploy the Templars is something that requires more than just my word. It has to be planned by Bishops or Cardinals. Moreover, think about this. Even if we were to dispatch Baifed and a couple of other Templars to your cause, we don't know what lies in wait for us on your homeworld. There could be battlemages or worse. Such matters take reconnaissance and planning. It could take years before we—"

"Years?" Anais nearly choked. "It's already been too long. Who knows what could happen to my family by then? I can't sit here for years on this awful desert world."

"Do not speak to Father Cline in such a manner," Baifed said.

"It's quite all right, my son," Father Cline said, his tone still measured. "She is distressed, and it's understandable." He turned to the table and paced, considering.

Anais wasn't sure whether to plead more or what she could say.

"Perhaps we could allow you to attempt to contact your world," Father Cline said. "I will contact the *Justicar*'s communication's officer and see what we can do."

Communications. That was something at least. Anais really wanted to get away from this world, but deep down, she understood Father Cline was correct. Trying to get ahold of someone back home would at least be a step in the right direction. "Thank you, Father," she said.

# THREE

DRIN CLUTCHED THE HANDRAIL AS THE TROOP TRANSPORT jolted. He stood with another dozen Templars, packed tightly together. The pilot had warned them there'd be turbulence. The upper atmosphere of Konsin II had heavy winds. One big drop made Drin's stomach lift to his throat, but he trusted the pilot to deliver them. The upcoming battle would be far more dangerous than the flight.

"Templars, prepare for drop," Commander Shayne shouted. He bowed his head. "Lord God on high, bless these warriors at your command. Let us do your will and bring only glory to your name. Vanquish the evils we are about to face and keep us free from harm and in your presence."

"Power and glory to Yezuah!" the Templars shouted in unison.

The craft landed with a *thud*, and the back ramp dropped open. The Templars formed armor from their nanites and ran out the back. Those in front fired laser-repeater rifles for suppression. Drin activated his light sword. It glowed a bright orange under the Konsin sun, shimmering as if the light itself were melting from the heat.

Thankfully, the nanites regulated his temperature. Sweat came from the nerves of battle, but the interior of his armor was comfortable. He looked ahead.

Though this area of the world was as much a desert as Altequine, the sands here had a red tint to them. Strange flat mesas surrounded the area in the distance, giving the city of Shiraz a naturally defensible position, at least in the age before flying vehicles.

Several other transports landed around the Templars, containing regular units from the *Justicar*, as well as support personnel.

Drin turned to the city. The walls were made of a shiny onyx with dozens of jagged points at the top. Beyond were three towers of similar build, jutting toward the sky like giant crystals. Sekaran guards stood on the wall in a line, and they opened fire, directing it all toward the Templars.

Several repeater bolts hit the front line, but the energy was absorbed by the nanites' shielding. The front line pressed forward, and Drin moved after them.

Drin broke into a run as he pushed toward the city wall. There were no open gates, but he didn't need one.

The support troops came from the side. Dozens of them carried large flat metallic contraptions called boosters. Handles on the sides of the boosters made them portable by a pair of soldiers, who held it in place for the Templars to use. They reached the walls just before Drin and the other Templars and set them at an angle. Drin ran toward one of the boosters and made sure to plant both feet on it when he made his last step.

The booster vibrated underneath his feet, and Drin leapt, launching high into the atmosphere. Drin flew through the air as high as the black crystal towers beyond. Then he began to descend. Drin pedaled his feet out of instinct, reaching for a footing not there. He came down at the perfect arc over the wall where the Sekaran line fired their ranged weaponry at the inbound Templars.

The enemy turned their laser-repeaters to Drin and six other Templars who floated through the air toward them. They fired. A bolt disintegrated into Drin's shielding, causing a pink light to flicker around him. The nanites couldn't deflect all of the force. It still hurt much like falling and hitting the ground. Drin winced, but such a small amount of pain was a pittance compared to what the bolts could do if they hit him without the shields.

He landed on top of the wall, spreading his arms for balance, his light sword active in one hand.

The Sekarans shouted, "Kill the infidels!"

Dozens of laser-repeater blasts targeted him. His shield kept up with the hits, but he wouldn't be able to sustain it against these levels of attacks for long. Drin charged, slashing at the Sekaran guards with his light sword. They met with instant death, the light sword cutting through their armor with ease.

Drin spun around to deal with the Sekarans on the opposite side of him. He took down two more guards, but one of the Sekarans had a shield of his own. Unlike the nanotechnology coursing through Drin's veins, this Sekaran had a device attached at his hip. He held onto a small rod, which he then activated into a light sword of his own.

A challenge.

Laser-repeater bolts still fizzled into the back of Drin's shield, but the others would have to deal with them. He had to face this Sekaran.

The Sekaran sword-wielder stepped forward, rotating the weapon in a brilliant display meant to intimidate. He handled the sword with finesse.

Drin wouldn't be intimidated by such tactics. He'd seen his share of battles with well-trained opponents over the years. He swung his blade with his full body's might.

The Sekaran blocked. The clash between the two light swords sent sparks flying all around them. The force made the Sekaran slip backward. "You are strong, Elorian, but strength isn't everything."

Drin's assault was met with a flurry of counterattacks. The Sekaran swung and stabbed, one attack after another in an impossibly fast rhythm. The assault forced Drin on the defensive, edging him backward. The enemy's sword skill was all too much, even for Drin.

Several of the Sekaran's assaults got past Drin's blocks, and his shield began to flicker. The light sword attacks created too much energy to absorb. Drin managed to push through the Sekaran's shield once, but his adversary left him very few openings.

Drin stepped back. His foot slipped on something, a protrusion that gave way. He lost his balance.

The Sekaran saw the opening and delivered a kick to the center of Drin's shielding. The shield flickered, dissipating, and the Sekaran's foot connected with Drin's hip. The shield slowed the blow, but already off-balance, Drin fell backward. He hit the hard onyx surface of the wall with enough force it would leave a nasty bruise.

His light sword winked out in the crash, a defensive reflex from the nanites so he wouldn't inadvertently cut his own limbs off.

Drin looked beside him to see what he had tripped over. It was a laser-repeater from one of the Sekaran guards he'd felled. The battlefield had become cluttered from his own early progress, and it proved his undoing. When he turned his attention back to the light sword-wielder, he saw the Sekaran looming, casting his shadow over him. The corona of the Konsin sun flickered behind the man's head like an artist's rendition of saints' halos.

The sight disturbed Drin. What if the Sekarans were right? If

Eltu were truly a prophet? Such doubt had never cluttered his mind before, but being faced with death shook him. It shouldn't...

*Lord Yezuah, forgive my sins and my doubt.*

"Die, Elorian blasphemer," the Sekaran said. He raised his light sword even higher, about to thrust it down and end Drin.

Another shadow darkened the sky. It distracted the Sekaran for the briefest of moments, causing him to look away.

Drin rolled to the right. When the Sekaran brought the light-sword down, it hit the onyx stone of the wall, sparking and kicking up pebbles as the blade dug into it.

The shadow disappeared, and a man's form landed behind the Sekaran. Drin scrambled backward, trying to get himself out of the path of the battle.

The Sekaran whirled in an effort to defend himself from this new attacker. Even with all his speed, though, his efforts proved futile.

The new figure had a light sword as well, and he had already begun his attack, pushing his whole strength into the blow, using his upper body to twist with perfect form. It burst through the Sekaran's shield, and the blow hit the shield's transmitter at the Sekaran's side. The shield flickered a translucent pink color similar to the one that surrounded Drin and the others.

The Sekaran jumped aside, barely having room on the top of the wall. His foot hit precariously close to the edge, but he recovered and faced his new attacker.

Drin recognized the newcomer to the battle: Jellal.

A sense of immense relief filled him, but Drin knew better than to relax in the middle of a battle, even with the odds of the situation changing. He grabbed the laser-repeater next to him and pointed it toward the pair.

Jellal and the Sekaran battled ferociously. Without the shield, the Sekaran wasn't so wild with his attacks but became more careful, parrying Jellal's assaults and keeping up blow for blow.

The two moved around far too much. Drin held the laser-repeater steady, but he couldn't get a clean opening between the two to shoot. Jellal kept getting in the way.

"Duck!" Drin shouted.

Jellal dropped to the onyx surface, not hesitating. The Templar brethren trusted each other implicitly, and that proved time and time again why they could be a superior fighting force to the Sekarans. Brotherly love conquered all.

The Sekaran grinned, no doubt believing he was going to be able to slaughter Jellal with ease as the Templar dropped to the floor. He ignored Drin, bringing up his light sword up again for a killing blow.

It gave Drin the opening he needed. He fired the laser-repeater three times, all of the bolts striking true into the Sekaran's chest.

Without the shield to deflect them, the bolts burnt holes through the man. He stumbled backward, scorched wounds evident in his chest. His jaw dropped, and he tried to speak, but he merely fell over backward, dead.

Jellal pushed himself to his feet with a grunt, his light sword having dissipated when he hit the ground. He dusted himself off and turned around to look at Drin. "Am I going to save you every time we go into battle from now on, brother?" He offered his hand.

Drin took the hand and the assistance up. "Maybe so," Drin said with humility. Jellal spoke in a light-hearted manner, but his words rang true. The last time they'd fought together, Drin struggled alone against a battlemage, and it took Jellal's help to finish off the villain. "I am glad to be back among the Templars. It's much better fighting with brothers at your side."

Jellal smiled and patted Drin on the shoulder. "That it is."

They both surveyed the battle scene. The Templars had secured Shiraz's front wall. Sekaran forces gathered below, having already set up sandbags and other obstacles to keep the Templars at bay. They would fight to the death, and this battle would be an intense one. A battlemage was down there somewhere in the city of Shiraz, and despite having a fairly bloodless victory in the first volley, they still had a lot of work to do.

The regular infantry below set up explosive charges, and the Templars up on the wall cleared the immediate area. Once everyone was in position, the infantrymen detonated the charges. It brought down a large section of the onyx wall, filling the air with black dust. The infantry flooded in through that hole, and laser-repeater fire blasted on both sides. Hundreds of bolts filled the air at the same time. The battle would begin in earnest at this point.

The Templars assembled together on opposite sides of the opening. They jumped off the wall in unison, landing together so they could charge forward along with the regular forces. "Glory to Yezuah!" several of the Elorian warriors shouted. They moved forward, overcoming the first line of the Sekarans battling against them.

The battle was going in their favor. The Lord had looked upon them with kindness on this day.

Drin pressed forward, slicing through several Sekaran soldiers with his light sword. Jellal and Commander Shayne flanked him, the three of them doing more damage than most of the infantry could as a combined force.

The area cleared as the Sekarans fell back into the city. Some of them took positions in windows, sniping at the invaders below. Different Elorian units broke off to clear the buildings.

There was still no sign of a battlemage. There had to be one here since Drin had been told there were two. He had already felled the other back in Altequine. The streets quieted. What was going on? Were the Sekarans going to cede this city to them? It seemed unlike them. Usually, their armies would fight to the death in the name of their false prophet.

Several moments passed. The sound of light repeater fire echoed through deadened streets. "Something's wrong," Drin said.

"I sense it, too," Jellal said.

Through the smoke and haze in the streets came a lone Sekaran. He didn't appear to be armed. A couple of the infantrymen fired at him, but he had one of the shields like the light sword-wielder on the wall. He would reach the Elorian line.

Drin couldn't understand the approaching Sekaran's gambit. The only result could be suicide.

Once the Sekaran came close enough to strike, Drin raised his light sword. After the laser-repeaters softened the attacker's shield, it would be easy to cut down this lone soldier. But at this close of range, Drin saw a twinkle in the Sekaran's eye, looking like he was pleased with the results of his charge.

Drin spotted the reason why the Sekaran had been so foolishly bold. The man had a detonator in his hand. He raised it in front of the Templars in an act of defiance. "I die in service to Eltu. And you will face a fiery hell, infidels," the Sekaran said.

He depressed his thumb on the detonator.

# FOUR

"STILL NO ANSWER ON THE INTERSTELLAR COMM," ANAIS said. She stood with Lyssa in a dimly lit room with a holodisplay on a round table. The holo had a circular icon which spun while the word "connecting" flashed above it. It hadn't changed for the last hour, despite their trying different comm frequencies.

The nuns had led them into this room and left them just before they made the call. The other Elorians still on the ship scrambled about the *Justicar* in a panic. They'd been that way since their attack on the Sekaran-controlled Shiraz earlier in the morning.

Drin had gone with them. Anais found herself stifling a breath when she thought of him.

"Are you okay?" Lyssa asked, an ear twitching with concern.

"Yeah, I'm fine. Just thinking about things I shouldn't."

"I know how it is. I'm thinking about my family, too," Lyssa said.

It wasn't what Anais had meant. Despite the fact Drin had spurned her advances several times, Anais still found herself attracted to him. Attracted was an understatement. She couldn't stop thinking about him. It drove her crazy. There was no future with him. He had a vow of celibacy to the church. They could never...

It was a waste of time for her to think about possible futures with him. She understood why he was on her mind. He battled out there, bravely liberating another city of Skree slaves and from Sekaran tyranny. It put him in danger, and it worried her.

She had to focus and find a way to communicate with her people back on Pyus. But how? If no one answered over the main trade channels or the Merchant Lord backchannel frequencies, did she have any other options? Even a general signal sent to the planet had been met with no response.

"What do we do?" Lyssa asked.

"I'm thinking," Anais said. She bit her lip, trying to remember if there were any other relevant comm frequencies she'd seen. It was so hard without the merchant lord familial databanks. It came to her. "Computer," she said, "contact the Parthenon Station in the Sagittarius sector."

The computer processed and found the general frequency for the station before trying to connect.

"Parthenon Station?" Lyssa asked.

Anais nodded. "I remember my father had a lot of trade contacts there. They act as a distribution hub bringing goods to and from Pyus."

"I think I remember hearing of it. I should have paid more attention to the family's business," Lyssa said.

"Me too, but we were young then." Though they hadn't aged much by time since they'd come to this godforsaken planet, their old lives felt like an eternity ago. Anais couldn't imagine herself going back to playing datapad games, shopping, and clubbing. She couldn't waste her time in this life any longer. Every moment was precious, every friendship and connection even more so. And it could all evaporate in a second. The hot, sandy world of Konsin proved a constant reminder of what she'd lost. "But if anyone knows what happened, it'd be—"

"Parthenon Station," someone answered the comm. The person had a squishy face with long eyes and a small wet nose, shining black through the comm system.

"Hi," Anais said, trying to sound dignified. "I am Anais from the Merchant Lord family Carver on Pyus. I'm calling to talk to our trading partners there on the station." She wished she'd remembered the name of their contact there, but maybe she could fake her way to someone important who would know what was going on. "I'm calling to talk to your CEO."

"One moment please," the person said. The image blinked to a logo of the station, rotating in front of them.

"They didn't hang up on you," Lyssa said.

"Nope," Anais agreed.

Another person of the same species came on the screen. This one had an orange streak to his fur. "Carver? Are you related to Olivar?"

"I'm his daughter," Anais said.

"Oh. You're alive." He sounded surprised.

"Of course I'm alive." Anais's heart fluttered. Did that mean her parents weren't any longer? It'd been something she'd feared for a long time, but she had no concrete evidence one way or another as to what had happened back on Pyus. The Sekarans were ruthless, but she still hoped her family was taken prisoner like she was, or left alone.

"My name is Nagell. Your father and I had many profitable business contracts over the years. I owe him a lot of what I've built here on Parthenon Station. I'm happy to help you as best I can, but I won't risk this station in getting involved in a full-scale conflict with the Sekarans," he said.

"I understand. I don't even know what happened on Pyus, though. I was taken and haven't been able to contact the world."

"I don't have many details, just what my trader captains have reported. There was an upheaval on Pyus where a small contingent of Sekarans sacked several of the merchant lords' homes. Most of my business contacts disappeared. At this point they're presumed dead, but then, so were you. Interesting."

He clicked his tongue. "But the Sekarans were galvanized by the quick way a small force could bring upheaval to your world. They invaded with their true force two weeks after the assault. We've seen what happens when they conquer worlds before, and as a trading hub, we stay away from those worlds. There have been enough trader ships not returning from Sekaran-controlled territory to make it too risky a venture. I wish I had more news for you."

Anais glanced to Lyssa. Having their world taken by the Sekarans was news to them. She'd hoped her capture had been an isolated incident. But it wasn't. She returned her attention to Nagell. "Thank you, it's a better start than we had before. I appreciate your time."

Nagell's eyes softened on the display. "I meant what I said about your father. If you want to come here, we can help you. If the Sekarans took you...I can't even imagine what was done to you. You'll be welcome here, and with the heritage of one of the merchant lords, I'm sure we could find employment for you."

"Thank you. It's a generous offer. I'm not sure what I'll do yet, but I'll be in contact."

"Good luck." Nagell cut the communication, and the image flickered out of existence.

Lyssa had tears streaking down her cheeks. "I can't believe they took our world. What are we going to do?"

Anais bit her lip. What could she do? She was just one person. "I don't know."

They relied on the Elorians, but the Elorians hadn't been willing to do much to help them. There was one who tended to be a little kinder to her than the others though: Drin. Anais prayed he made it back from his current battle alive.

# FIVE

THE SEKARAN EXPLODED, SCREAMING TO HIS FALSE PROPHET Eltu before the blast took him. The detonation engulfed the front lines of the Elorian troops. A shockwave shot forward, heat and wind forcing Drin to avert his eyes.

His nanite shield flickered and then dropped from existence. He couldn't feel the nanites inside of him. Drin panicked, trying to summon a light sword into his hand.

Nothing.

This had been the Sekarans' ploy. Dozens of them advanced from deeper inside the city, marching down the main road.

Drin tried to create his light sword again. Still nothing. He glanced to Jellal. "The nanites—"

Jellal frowned, holding his hands out as if that would make them come back. "I don't sense anything either. It must have been some sort of EMP blast."

Without the nanites, they were in dire straits, though not completely helpless. They'd been trained to fight without technological assistance from a young age. "Never rely on your nanites," his master said during sword training. "You never know what will happen in the course of a battle."

He'd been right. This wasn't the first time Drin had no access to his nanites. He recalled a fight against a battlemage in Altequine where they'd been overwhelmed, but this was different. Then, he could be sure the nanites would return. Now...

"Now, we have to take these Sekaran weapons and join the others. They will need every last man, nanites or not," Drin said, motioning to the weapons by their fallen enemies.

Jellal picked up a laser-repeater, handed it to Drin, and then took one for himself. He knelt at the Sekaran's physical light sword. "Do you want it, or me?"

Drin frowned, considering. Who would be the best person to use the light sword? Jellal was often faster, but Drin felt he was better with precision strikes. They didn't have time to delay and think on it, however. "Give it to me," he said.

"I shouldn't have asked," Jellal said, handing Drin the weapon.

Further down the street, soldiers on both sides clashed. Laser-repeater fire blasted through the air again. They had to reach their fellow soldiers and assist. It was a complete frenzy, and these laser-repeaters wouldn't be accurate enough to hit the correct targets from here.

"Let's go," Drin said. They came across four other Templars along the way, and soon Drin had a good portion of his unit behind him. "Are all of your nanites gone, too?" The others nodded. They would be regular infantry for the duration of this battle. Drin hoped the nanites wouldn't be gone from their systems permanently—if they survived.

The Templars took a circuitous route to the main fighting, hoping to flank the enemy. The outer road curved around several buildings, and they came to a side street, where a Sekaran unit ran toward the main battle. The enemy hadn't spotted them.

"We'll have them trapped," Drin said, holding his unit back on the stairs so they wouldn't push further into the Sekarans' view.

Once the Sekarans disappeared down the street, Drin motioned to his men. They moved forward like clockwork. Even without nanites, they had gone to battle together so many times before, they knew what to do. These were truly his brothers. It felt good not to be fighting alone any longer.

The Templars turned the corner where the Sekarans had just passed. The enemy had their backs to them, faced toward the battle ahead. Drin waited until all of his men were in position, leveled his laser-repeater, and then opened fire.

The other Templars fired with him, their laser bolts striking true. By the time the Sekarans turned around, two-thirds of them were dead. Four remained. Their shots blasted back at the Templars.

A laser bolt hit Illenum on the shoulder. He clutched it as he collapsed into the street.

"Take cover!" Drin shouted.

The Templars fell back, using the buildings and inset door-ways to hide from the return fire. They kept shooting. Drin knocked another down. Jellal hit another.

The other two Sekarans fled, placing their laser-repeaters under their arms and firing back as they ran. Their shots went wild. Drin placed his arms out to steady his aim, but two of the other Templars hit his targets before he could get a good shot.

The Templars secured the area around Illenum. Drin bent down on a knee beside him. "Brother," he said.

"Hurts..." Illenum said.

The wound looked pretty bad. The laser-repeater fire cauter-ized, but it blew a sizable hole in Illenum's shoulder. If either of them had nanites, they could heal the debilitating blow, but they didn't have the luxury. They had no means to do anything about the wound. At the very least, Illenum would be unable to fight with them. If they left him in the street, however, he would be certain to die.

Drin glanced to a building. He pointed. "Knock out that window. We're going to move Illenum inside so he's out of the street. He can't come with us, but we have to help the others. We don't want more Sekaran patrols coming across him in the street. Move."

The others knocked the window out with the butts of their laser-repeaters, and then came back to move Illenum. The four Templars lifted him, each by one limb. Illenum grunted with each step. He turned pale.

"I'm sorry we can't stay with you, brother Illenum. We will be back for you or die first. I vow this," Drin said.

"I know, brother. Glory to Yezuah. I pray for His mercy," Illenum said as another Templar set him down.

"Let's go," Drin said. As much as he wanted to dote on his brother, there were others waiting for them. And if they didn't win the battle ahead, Illenum's life would be moot anyway.

They continued down the street, keeping their laser-repeaters trained and their eyes peeled. The sound of weapons fire echoed through the empty streets. They would be coming up upon the main battle soon. The noises became louder, coupled with the grunts of death.

Shouts came from behind them.

Another squad of Sekarans advanced. Drin motioned for his men to fan out across the street and take cover again. They were in a commercial area, with several abandoned vehicles and shop carts. It made it easier to hide. Sweat dripped down Drin's face. Without the nanites, he no longer had a temperature control. The heat of the desert was beginning to get to him. His mouth dried, and he smacked his lips trying to get them some moisture. He needed water, but he didn't have time to think on it.

Laser-repeater bolts came toward the Templars, blasting the

ground in front of them and their cover. Drin ducked into an alleyway just beyond one building, pressing up against it. Both sides engaged in heavy fire, but, out of the corner of his eye, Drin spotted something moving.

A figure moved down a parallel street, where Drin's alley connected. The figure had a long, flowing cape and a shaved head with a metallic protrusion on his forehead. The battlemage.

The battlemage didn't spot Drin. He kept focused toward the main battle just a few blocks further.

Drin wanted to call out to the other Templars. This was their primary target. If they could take the battlemage down, it would cripple the Sekarans. Even without the nanites, they would have a better chance. And reinforcements would be able to arrive later to give them better strength. The Sekarans couldn't hold Shiraz forever without their battlemage.

Even though Drin had an obligation to his brothers, he had to break off for the greater battle. Guilt swelled in him for not being able to call out to his brethren, but he couldn't risk alerting the battlemage to his presence. Not in his current condition. Even with nanites, it would be a tough battle, but without, he had to rely on stealth to get the job done.

He crept down the alley, staying concealed in the shadows of the buildings. He kept his laser-repeater pointed forward in case he ran into any other trouble on the way. The Sekaran light sword dangled from his belt, clipped there.

At the corner, Drin stopped. He glanced to the street beyond. The battle raged in front of him. Sekarans battled hand-to-hand with Elorian regulars, and likely some of the Templars from the other side of the wall.

The two forces looked equally matched, but the battlemage made all the difference. The Sekaran wizard focused and lifted into the air, his palms down, as if pushing himself upward by his will. Drin knew it was technology the Sekarans had, a heretical mockery of the nanites Yezuah had bestowed on the Elorians. Heresy or no, it had an impact.

The sight gave the Elorian front lines pause, one in which the Sekarans took advantage. Several Elorian soldiers fell to blasts and knife attacks. Then the battlemage began his attack in earnest.

From his hands, the battlemage formed balls of energy, which he threw toward the Elorians. The energy was strong, blasting in a radius that took out three or more Elorians with each explosion. The battlemage kept forming energy and kept throwing, one arm after another. He would decimate the Elorians if someone didn't do something soon.

Drin had the opportunity.

A laser-repeater blast likely wouldn't get past the battlemage's shields, but he had a second weapon.

Drin dropped the pistol and grabbed the Sekaran light sword from his hip. It was heavy, not a simple extension of his will like the light sword formed by the nanites. The heaviness bothered him, but Drin was proficient with metal swords as well as his people's holy blade. He activated the light sword, the blade shimmering to life in front of him.

The battlemage was up in the air, higher than a standard person could jump. Drin would have been able to boost himself with his nanites, but he would have to rely on his own strength and pray it was enough. He had little choice. He had to try.

Determined, Drin rushed to a running start. One foot padded after the next as he gained speed in an attempt to come up upon the battlemage. So far, the battlemage seemed preoccupied, throwing energy ball after energy ball, not bothering to look behind him and ascertain if there were any threats.

At full speed, Drin approached from behind. One of the Sekarans at the line above spotted him and called out to the battlemage.

With an energy ball fully formed in his hand, the battlemage turned just as Drin leaped to meet him. Drin lifted his sword high over his head to deliver a mighty blow with all of his forward momentum. The battlemage tried to counter by throwing the energy ball.

The ball fizzled by Drin's head, narrowly missing.

Drin's swing struck with the full force of his muscular arms. It burst through the battlemage's shield as if it weren't there, and sliced straight through the Sekaran's body. Hovering in the air, the Sekaran flailed as he was cut into two pieces. A second energy ball fizzled in his hands as he fell to the ground.

Drin barely managed to land on his feet, surprised his attack had worked so well. He had been fully prepared to die, even to fail. But his action turned the tide of the battle.

The Elorians cheered. The battlemage was dead. It would be a matter of time now until they declared victory.

Drin had to get out of the way as the Sekarans at the back of their line turned their attentions to him. He scrambled backward and dove for the alley. Laser bolts seemed to be everywhere around him at once, but amazingly none hit him. He skidded across the ground, feeling his skin chafe and burn from the maneuver, but he'd made it to cover.

Jellal pulled him to his feet. His team was there. "We've got you covered. Smooth move out there. You're almost as good a swordsman as me," Jellal said. He and the others rounded the corner of the building and turned their laser-repeaters on the Sekarans. The enemy was flanked and had no powerful commander any longer.

Shiraz would fall to the Elorians, and the planet Konsin would be freed in its entirety.

# SIX

Anais watched the sun set, red hues streaking across the sky. She'd been waiting for the Elorians to get back from their mission to the other side of this world. Her ear twitched. Nerves. Would Drin be okay? She had no reason to think otherwise. Every time he'd been present, he acted as the one constant that seemed unstoppable. Except when the battlemage had nearly killed him, but that was out of his control.

A few small dots appeared over the horizon. As they came closer, they grew. Boxy shapes cast shadows over the sands as they moved. They finally came into clear view: Elorian troop transports.

Thrusters blared when they came close, blowing wind and kicking up dust, causing Anais to have to avert her eyes. The shuttle hangar of the *Justicar* was several levels above where she stood. They'd land there.

Anais jogged up the ramp of the ship to make her way up the half-dozen levels to greet them. Not them, only one Elorian among them. Drin. If he had survived the journey.

When she arrived at the hangar, hundreds of Elorians exited

the crafts. They looked nearly indistinguishable, all in their armor, worn from a long day of fighting. But the people exiting wore regular armor, not the shining glow of the Templars' nanite fields. Anais stood on the tips of her toes to see if she could spot Drin and the others.

Several Templars exited one craft toward the back. Anais stepped to the side to allow the other Elorians to pass. She'd been waiting for a few hours, it wouldn't hurt to be patient for a little longer. Her heart raced with anticipation.

One by one, the Templars exited the shuttle. She spotted Baifed, who she wasn't looking forward to speaking with again, but no Drin so far. The ramp hung down, empty. No others came.

The Templars walked by. Baifed stopped and narrowed his eyes when he passed Anais. "What are you doing here?" he asked.

"I'm hoping to see Templar Drin," Anais said. "Is he...?"

A lump grew in her throat. She didn't want to admit that something could have happened to him.

Baifed looked at her as if she were crazy. "He's in the shuttle. He took a laser-repeater blast to the thigh in the final assault. He's having trouble moving."

"You didn't stay with him to help him?" Anais asked.

Baifed laughed, jovial for once. "Have you met Templar Drin? I'd like to see *you* try to offer him assistance."

He actually made Anais smile. "I think I will." She nodded to him and trudged over to the craft, where the ramp still lingered, hanging down to the flight deck.

Drin stood at the entry, limping. A scorch marred his leg, looking like the laser bolt carved out a chunk of muscle. The grimace on his face told Anais he suffered tremendous pain.

Anais made her way up the ramp and tried to maneuver into a place where he could lean on her.

"I can walk on my own," Drin said.

"No, you can't, stubborn."

He sighed and put an arm around her shoulder. Anais managed to sneak a closer glance at the wound. The torn muscle and caked blood looked like a mess.

"What happened?" she asked.

"The Sekarans had some kind of EMP bomb. It knocked out all of our nanotechnology. We had to fight without any of our protections."

"Sounds dangerous." Anais slowly moved down the ramp, letting Drin set the pace as he hobbled.

"It was. Fortunately, I managed to sneak up on the battlemage. I have to speak with Father Cline and see if there's a way to rejuvenate the nanites within us. If we can't get them working again..." he shook his head.

Anais didn't know what to say, so she bit her lip. They reached the bottom of the ramp. It would take hours to walk out of the hangar at this rate. She should have called for a stretcher, or a wheelchair, or something to carry Drin. But he would balk at the suggestion. Was there something else she could try? He didn't have the nanites anymore, but they coursed through her veins. She'd failed earlier when Baifed attempted to show her how to heal, but she'd done it once before in a pinch. She could do it again. "I want to try to heal you."

"No need," Drin said.

"Please?" She looked up at him with big eyes.

Drin grimaced. She'd seen that look before. One where he didn't like it, but he was bound to give into her. "Fine," he said.

Anais moved him to the side of the craft so he could lean on it while she looked at his leg. She crouched beside the wound. How did it work? The nanites operated on will, didn't they?

She took a deep breath, calming herself, trying to feel the little tech flowing through her. She couldn't feel anything, but she knew they were there. She had to do this. For Drin.

Raising her hands, she tried to visualize a healed leg. The

nanites could repair it. It was all faith, wasn't it? She'd had little faith in them when she'd tried to heal the Skree, but this was more important. She pressed her hands against the wound. Drin winced, but kept his jaw shut. She couldn't imagine him crying or screaming from a wound. With one more deep breath through her nose, Anais pushed her will with all of her thoughts toward the wound, repairing it, healing. Her focus was intense, nothing else clouded her mind. She would do this.

Green light flashed from her hands. It swelled into a bubble around Drin's thigh, so bright she had to turn her head to the side to avert her eyes. It felt like something was sucking her very life out of her. It stung like an insect bit her repeatedly all the way through her arms and up to her spine. She heard herself whimper, but her body felt disconnected from her being in the moment. It was an unfamiliar sensation, but it was almost as if her soul was pulled from her body like a band and snapped back.

The glow faded. Anais felt dizzy and nearly fell to the floor.

Drin caught her.

He'd moved with full speed when he did. When he righted both her and himself, he no longer had any limp. He looked her in the eyes with those deep, dark pools, searing with their attention. Eyes Anais could get lost in forever. "You did it. Incredible," he whispered.

He held her close, and his sturdy muscular arms were the only thing that kept her from falling. Anais smiled wide. "I did it," she repeated.

"Let's get you to the med bay now and make sure there's nothing wrong with you. That seemed to take a lot out of you."

"Whatever you say," Anais said. She still felt dizzy, almost drunk. Drin lifted her to her feet and righted her.

"Hold on," Drin said. He stepped back from her. Anais was careful to keep her balance when he moved aside. An expression of intense concentration crossed his face. Little dots of light formed all around him like a field, and soon, the cloth of Drin's simple clothing became the Templar armor, thick and hard as a rock. "You did more than just heal my wound, you righted the nanites within me. No wonder you were so drained."

"That's good news. The battle went well, aside from the nanite issue?"

Drin linked his arm with hers, making sure she was steady as they walked. "We lost Illenum," Drin said.

"I don't think I met him," Anais said. "Were you close?"

"He was a brother."

They made their way out of the hangar. Only the techs were left there now, the soldiers all having gone to showers.

By the time they made it out of the hangar, into the winding corridors of the ship, Anais's head had cleared. She could take a good, long nap and feel a lot better, but at least she had her wits about her again. "I don't think I need to go to medical. I'm recovered," she said.

Drin glanced at her, looking her over as if scrutinizing her. "You do seem to be standing on your own two feet," he said, promptly unhooking his arm from hers.

"I wanted to talk to you, actually."

"About your homeworld?" Drin asked.

"How did you know?"

"You've been itching to get back since we met, and understandably so." He frowned, his forehead wrinkling. "What's the status on your world?"

"I don't know. I attempted to call on all channels, but I couldn't reach anyone."

"The Sekarans could be jamming the signal."

"Yeah..." *Or there could be no one left alive.* The thought sent chills down her spine.

"No information on the nets?"

Anais shook her head. "Not that I could find. Lyssa is scouring for information, but neither of us have many contacts outside of our world. I managed to speak to the head of Parthenon Station. He says the Sekarans have taken the world and most of the galactic traders are avoiding Pyus because of that."

"That's bad news," Drin said.

"Yeah."

They walked along the hall in silence. Other voices mumbled down other branches, the sound muffled by the sound of the air vents pumping recycled air into the ship. It was much cooler in here than out in the Konsin sun.

"Have you spoken to Father Cline?" Drin asked after they made their way down the hall. Anais wasn't sure where he led them, but she figured she would walk with him until he dismissed her, at least.

"I tried, but he wouldn't listen to me. That's part of why I wanted to talk to you. I was hoping you might be able to try to convince him?" She tilted her head at him, fluttering her long eyelashes. Both of them stopped in their step.

Drin's lips tightened. He looked at her in the deep manner he often did, as if he were searching her soul. The look used to bother Anais, but now she found it comforting. It was his way of caring. "I'm not sure I could convince him beyond what your own passionate pleas were able to accomplish."

"He thinks it's too dangerous, that a deeper plan of attack needs to be made. He says strategizing could take years."

"He's right."

Tears welled, though Anais tried to hold them back. "But my parents...my sisters...my friends."

Drin averted his eyes. "Let's go speak with Father Cline."

He would help. Hope filled Anais. As much as Drin said Father Cline wouldn't be persuaded by his words, the Templar fraternity was a tight one. They listened to each other.

The two rounded a corner and made their way to the sanctuary where Anais had seen Father Cline the last time. The doors were open, several Templars and others knelt in prayer, muttering thanks to Yezuah for their recent victory.

Father Cline was among them, in the front row rather than up on the dais. Something about the fact that the high priest prayed with the other worshipers rather than lording over them made Anais comfortable. She hadn't been sure about a God existing before all of this. When imprisoned by the Sekarans, she was downright sure He didn't exist, but Drin and the others convinced her otherwise. Besides, with all the miracles she'd witnessed, it would be impossible for the universe not to have a plan.

Drin sidestepped into one of the pews and knelt, leaving enough room for Anais to do the same beside him. She did so. He muttered prayers in a voice so low she couldn't understand.

"Father God," Anais started to say, but stopped. She glanced to either side, wondering who might be listening—judging her words. She swallowed and tried again, but this time no words would come out. The Elorians all seemed able to find words and just flow as if the prayer were a part of them. She only had few words. It was better to keep them silent. *God, if you're there, help me find my people. Help me save them.*

After she thought the short prayer, she waited. The others took a long time. After a time, Father Cline stood and took note of Drin and her. He walked to the rear pews and motioned to them.

Drin stood. Anais followed. They both fell into a single file line behind Father Cline, leaving the sanctuary and entering a small office across from where the others knelt in prayer.

"Brother Drin, I'm informed you did well today. Without your efforts, our holy forces might have been wiped out."

"I did my part as one of many," Drin said.

How did he stay so humble? Anais didn't know what happened in the battle, but when he spoke like he did, she knew there had to be more to it.

"But you did not come to me to speak of today's battle, did you?" Father Cline said. He glanced between them, knowingly.

How did the Templars all have an uncanny way of understanding exactly what she was going to say before she said it? Perhaps they did get some wisdom from on high.

"No, we did not," Drin agreed.

"You know I can't authorize sending the *Justicar* into battle. It's beyond my station. Besides, we need to ensure Konsin stays secure. We just captured the planet from the Sekarans today. Leaving would be—"

Alarms sounded. He paused his speech, looking up at red lights that flashed in the office.

Anais tensed. What was going on? "Drin?" She asked.

"We're under attack," Drin said.

# SEVEN

"Bridge," Father Cline said, tapping into the *Justicar's* internal comm system.

Drin stood, watching with Anais. The alert lights kept flashing, and the alarms still sounded. Anais looked even paler than she usually did, but Drin wouldn't panic.

"Bridge here. Father Cline?" A voice came through the comm.

"What's the situation?"

"Sekarans jumped out of hyperspace. They'll be in orbit in ten minutes."

"Prepare the *Justicar* for launch. If we're dirtside, we'll be sitting ducks."

"Yes, Father."

Father Cline looked to Drin, making clear his words were meant for him as well as the person on the bridge listening in through the comm. "We'll have to scramble our fighters. We don't want the Sekarans making landfall and erasing all of the good we've done here. I was hoping we'd have more time to settle Konsin, but it was a matter of time before they decided to send a fleet. Ready for lift-off and battle."

"Yes, Father," the bridge officer said. The comm chimed and turned off.

Father Cline laid a hand on Drin's shoulder. "Brother Drin, I know you're fresh from battle, but we have need of you and the Templars again. We'll need to get the civilians debarked as quickly as we can and get to the ship." He turned to Anais. "Please, exit the ramp as quickly as you can, and bring your other Pyus friend with you."

"I'm staying here," Anais said.

Father Cline inclined his head. "My daughter, please, now is not the time."

"You have injured from the battle that need tending to, don't you? I can heal them." Anais crossed her arms.

"Brother Baifed said you failed in healing—"

Anais pointed to Drin. "I can heal. Ask him."

Drin glanced between the two. Father Cline clearly wanted an excuse to get Anais off the ship, but he couldn't lie. "Yes, she healed me on the way here. She's making progress with control of her nanites. Speaking of which, I don't know if it's been reported to you, but the Templars involved in the battle were hit with some sort of EMP blast. Our nanites were knocked out. We just left the bay, so I think the others still have theirs deactivated."

"But yours are fine?" Father Cline raised a brow.

"Anais revitalized them somehow," Drin said. "She is an asset to us."

Father Cline sighed. "Fine. She can stay. We don't have time to argue, and I need to get to the bridge to direct the battle." He set his eyes upon Anais. "It will be dangerous aboard the *Justicar* these next few hours. I cannot guarantee your safety. Try to stay out of the way of the fighting crew and engineering teams. You should head to the medical bay and assist the sisters there."

"Okay," Anais said. She looked like a scared child.

"Attend to your duties," Father Cline said, dismissing them. "Glory to Yezuah."

"Glory to Yezuah," Drin said. He bowed slightly before Father Cline, then turned. Anais followed his lead. Soon, they were out in the corridor again, where several of the ship's crew rushed to their battle stations. "Do you remember where the medical bay is?" Drin asked Anais.

"Yeah, I think so."

"Good. I will have to do my duty and fly one of the fighters. I cannot watch you," he said. In some ways, he regretted leaving her. Anais was so new in the faith and seemed so lost without him. None of the others could shepherd her like he could. Was it because she still had latent feelings for him?

He had told her under no uncertain terms of his vow of celibacy, but the way she stood there, looking up at him, her eyes wide and so bright... Did she still love him? Drin didn't want to think of it. He turned his head away. "I need to get going."

"I know. Good luck," Anais said.

"Yezuah bless you," Drin said emphatically. There would be no luck involved in the battle. The outcome would be whether the Lord blessed them in victory or had other plans. Drin turned and jogged down the corridor to make his way back to the flight deck.

When he arrived, several of his brothers were already there. Commander Shayne paced in front of the Templars, where they stood at attention. Err-dio, one of the six-armed inhabitants of this planet, the Skree, stood with them. What was he doing here?

"We're going back into battle. I know you're tired, that the nanites aren't working or giving you strength," Commander Shayne said, "but when we are called to fight on behalf of the Lord, we must answer the call. He will give rest for the weary upon his return. We will know the joys of being with him in the flesh, just as the nanites give us a small hint of what is to come. It's his will that you operate as you do now."

They didn't know Drin had been healed, his nanites functioning again because of Anais. It would be better if they could be healed as well, but there wasn't time. He decided not to say anything about it. Drin stood at attention, body straight, falling into line with the others.

"All hands, prepare for lift-off," a voice came through the comm, echoing across the flight deck. Drin could feel the rumble of the engines lifting off beneath his feet. The *Justicar* took flight. He looked out the end of the hangar, where a forcefield kept them safely inside, away from the elements. At least they were in a location where he could see. He preferred to have a sense of where he was going.

The desert below became a mere patch of brown within moments. The buildings of Altequine dwindled to dots and then faded. They would be in space soon.

Commander Shayne brought a hand to his ear, where he could listen to his private comm. "Report from the bridge. The Sekarans will be here in five minutes. Everyone, get to your fighters, stat! Power and glory to Yezuah!"

"Power and glory to Yezuah," the Templars said in unison.

They broke off and made for their individual fighters, all except for Err-dio, who stopped in front of Drin.

"Brother Drin," Err-dio said, waving three of his arms on one side of his body.

"What are you doing with us?" Drin asked. Err-dio had been at the side of his planet's king, Sao-rin, since Drin had first met them. The Sekarans had been planning to stone all of them at the time. The Skree people had come far since their enslavement.

"I have piloting skills, so I offered to help fight the good fight. This is what the faith is for, to use our gifts for Him, yes?" Err-dio asked.

"True. I'm surprised they are letting you. I mean no offense, but it's odd to have a non-Elorian on one of our ships."

"Father Cline said the Templars were down a few pilots since the last battle. I offered to apprentice so I could grow in the faith, and because I wanted to follow you."

Drin froze in place. "I'm not sure I am one to follow—"

"You saved my people, Brother Drin. I may never have nanites as you do, but I can, at the very least, act as a squire. There is precedent in the holy book for—"

Commander Shayne cleared his throat. "Save the theological discussion for another time. You need to get to your vipers!"

"Sorry," Err-dio said. "Do the Lord proud, brother. I will be at your side, and you can count on me."

Drin nodded, and, without further word, jogged over to his viper. He climbed the ladder and slid into the seat. It'd been a while since he'd sat at the controls of a fighter. The only vehicle he'd had to pilot over the last several months was one of Konsin's desert sky-bikes. Those had very limited controls compared to a viper. He ran his hands over the two joysticks. They felt so familiar, despite his absence. It was good the Templars had been able to recover his craft from when he crashed in the Konsin desert. He pressed the controls to seal the cockpit hatch. It made a *whoosh* noise as it pressurized.

"Elorians, this is Sao-rin, King of Konsin and of the free Skree," Sao-rin said. "Your leaders have added me to your fleet's communications channels. We will be providing ground defense and assistance from the liberated orbital platforms the Sekarans put into place. We have the controls and the codes. They'll be surprised to find this world is fortified, not for them, but on behalf of the true God. May He bless you this day and protect this world and its people."

Drin was happy to hear the Skree king. Depending on the size of fleet the Sekarans sent, they would need all the help they could get. Bright lights flashed on the flight deck to signal that it was about to be depressurized. It looked like everyone had vacated the hangar. The *Justicar* had drilled and fought enough that their people worked like clockwork. They were as efficient a fighting force as one could ask for. As Drin turned on his viper's engines, he hoped the Elorian forces would be enough to resist the Sekarans.

# EIGHT

ANAIS WOUND HER WAY AROUND THE GIANT ELORIAN SHIP. She vaguely remembered the medical bay's location, but she had spent most of her time there as a patient. Everyone in the corridors seemed in a rush, tense. The atmosphere put Anais on edge, even though there was nothing she could do about the incoming Sekaran fleet.

When she finally found the proper room, an area with two frosted glass doors opening automatically upon her arrival, Anais found the medical bay was bustling with people just as frantic as those outside. More than a dozen injured Elorians lay on cots. Doctors and nurses tended to the worst of them, while other patients had bot attendants injecting painkillers.

The medical bay looked sleek, with plenty of modern instruments and computers. The care in here had to be better than anything the soldiers could receive outside of the ship, but still, the doctors raced against time in some instances.

"We're losing one," a doctor said, smock covering his face. "I'm going to need a stimulator. His heart's not beating anymore!"

One of the nurses rushed over with a small electronic device in her hand. It was the older woman, Vith, who had attended to Anais before. She handed the small device to the doctor, who set it on the injured Elorian's chest.

The man's chest didn't rise and fall but held still. Drool dripped down his face, and his eyes were open, rolled back in his head.

The doctor placed the device on his chest. "Go," he said.

The device jolted the Elorian on the table. His whole body shook.

"Someone hold him down!" The doctor shouted. Several attendants grabbed his arms and legs.

"Another," the doctor said. The device shook him again. The monitors showed a small beat of the heart. It restarted his system. The Elorian breathed, but only shallowly. "He's still in critical condition," the doctor said. "I'm not sure what we can do."

"Pray," Vith said.

"You do that. I'll move to the next patient," the doctor said. He turned for the next table, where another Elorian was covered in blood. Even his bandages had nearly been bled through.

Anais stepped forward carefully. Vith muttered prayers to herself. Anais didn't want to interrupt, but she thought she could help the patient whose heart had just been restarted. She'd healed Drin, after all. She could do it again, in theory. She placed her hands on the man.

"What are you doing?" Vith asked.

"I'm healing."

"Are you sure you know what you're doing?" the Elorian woman narrowed her eyes.

"No, but if I don't try, he's probably going to die anyway, right?"

Vith looked like she was going to protest but, instead, nodded. "Your heart is in the right place, and your faith in your abilities is strong. You do have the Lord's technology in your veins. I'll defer to you."

"Thanks," Anais, said. She concentrated on the man. She wasn't even sure where this man's wounds were, but it was hurting his ability to breathe. He'd lost a lot of blood. Anais directed the nanites to repair the wound. It shouldn't have been difficult. She breathed in and out as she concentrated, trying to visualize the man as healthy and sitting up on the table.

Energy flowed through her. Anais stifled a breath. It was almost too much, overwhelming. Soon, the glowing light of working nanites flowed over the man like a blanket.

Vith stepped back. "Blessings," she muttered to herself.

The energy continued for a time. It seemed a little less draining than when she had interacted with Drin. But she had also restored his nanites, didn't he say? This was an ordinary soldier, not one of the Templars. The Templars would all be in their fighter ships.

Anais narrowed her eyes. She didn't want to lose her concentration by worrying about what she couldn't control. She breathed in through her nose slowly, refocusing on the man.

The light dwindled. Anais stepped back. "I think...I think I did it," she said. Oddly, she was out of breath. Dizzy, like last time, but not to the point where she needed help standing.

Vith checked the instruments for the man's vitals. "He does appear to have stabilized. We'll have to monitor him."

The doctor circled back to the table, frowning at the vitals. "She appears to have the gift. I've only seen a Templar perform such miracles," he said before moving to the next patient.

"Can you help the others?" Vith asked.

Anais nodded. "I need a break, though. Somewhere to sit. And some water, please."

"We'll get it for you. Take the chair right over there," Vith said. She motioned to the chair and waddled away from the bed.

The healed man stirred and groaned. He rolled to his side.

Anais carefully moved to the chair and let herself fall into it. The room still spun to some degree. She touched her forehead as if that would help her steady herself. She could heal. This was an incredible gift. For the first time in her life, she felt as if she had some purpose. She'd been drifting before, from clubs and school back on Pyus, to following Drin around, and she'd never found herself to be any use to those around her.

These new abilities changed everything. It filled her with joy. Was this what it felt to experience God like Drin prattled on about? If it was, she wanted more of it.

Vith returned with a glass of water and a very old book. It had a worn leather cover, and some of the pages were torn. She handed both to Anais.

"What's this?" Anais asked.

"This is a copy of The Gospel of Marayh. It's not part of our holy canon but considered apocrypha." She tilted her head at Anais. "I see you're confused by the terms. Worry not, you'll learn them in time. It means we can't verify who the author of the work was, though it does claim to be by the saint herself. It's a series of letters regarding her travels and healing. Maybe you'll find some use in it. Perhaps you are the beginning of a new order."

Anais gulped down some of the water, realizing then how dry her mouth had been. Her? A founder of some new order of nuns? She was hardly worthy of the consideration. "I don't know," Anais said.

"Take your time. Patience is the key to God's love," Vith said.

"Is that from the Holy Book?"

Vith nodded. "Indeed. It's stated several times. I should get back to my duties. Drink. Rest. Read. When you're ready, there are more men who require your attention. They're not in as bad of condition as the one you already saved, but we could use your help."

Anais cracked open the old book, careful not to cause any more damage to it. The words were handwritten. This had to be very valuable. "Okay," she said, looking up to Vith. "You can count on me."

# NINE

THE GRAVITATIONAL FORCE JOLTED DRIN INTO THE SEAT OF his viper. It'd been a while since he'd taken off in one of these. The thrill of flying made his blood pump hard through his veins. Blood with functioning nanites again, praise Yezuah. He owed Anais so much. She'd saved his life once, and now she had restored him to be able to fight once more. Not that he'd need the nanites in this space battle. He had navigational and targeting AIs to assist him.

Drin flew through open space. Stars blanketed the dark sky like milky streaks. If he had to rely on vision alone, he wouldn't have been able to spot the enemy battleship ahead of him—a black mass, a mere shadow in the sky. But his computer locked in on the battleship, which stretched across his targeting screen like the devil's own hand. Sekaran fighters scrambled from the vessel, looking like a swarm of insects. Evil incarnate.

A flurry of laser fire came from the enemy, but it wasn't targeting individual fighters. The Sekarans took aim for the *Justicar.* Drin managed to avoid the bolts shooting in his direction. He targeted the lead Sekaran fighters.

"Stay in formation," Commander Shayne said through the

comm. He pushed his viper out front, just to the right of Drin's. The Templars split their fighters into wings, and tried to stick together as best as possible. It made it easier to target and pick off enemies and also provided some useful backup if there was a problem.

They engaged the enemy. Drin fired his lasers on the Sekaran fighters, managing to connect with one. Several of the other Elorian fighters followed his targeting, and the first casualty of the battle was claimed. The Sekaran ship blew to bits. On to the next one.

Far too many Sekaran fighters followed, outnumbering the Elorian ships. It was hard to tell who was who in the heat of the dogfight. They swarmed, cluttering this area of space. Drin did all he could to evade their fire, connecting with several Sekaran ships with his own. The Sekaran fleet made up for the Elorian firepower and maneuverability with sheer numbers.

"I've got two of them on my tail!" Baifed shouted through the comm.

Drin looked at his nav to see where Baifed's ship was, and he tapped in a command to follow his brother. His viper whirled around looping from top to bottom, flipping to change the local vertical. The internal gravity of the cockpit kept Drin from feeling much different, but it still had a dizzying effect on his eyes as he adjusted to upside down being the new right side up.

"I'm coming for you," Drin said through the comm as he tried to ascertain Baifed's position. He spotted the silver Elorian viper up ahead, and sure enough, it had two Sekaran ships following behind. Baifed was under heavy fire.

Drin managed to get a lock on one Sekaran immediately, scoring a direct hit on its engine. The enemy fighter spun out of control, veering off toward below the bottom hull of the *Justicar*. Only one ship mattered now.

The remaining Sekaran fired more shots and managed to clip

Baifed's wing. The Elorian viper wobbled, but Baifed was able to steady the ship with a couple of adjustment thrusts.

Drin fired again, but this one proved better at evading shots. It barrel-rolled left and right. Frustrating how it managed to predict all of Drin's fire.

Another laser bolt hit Baifed's viper. Drin held his breath when a small flash erupted at the back of the ship. Would this one prove fatal to his brother?

While the shot distracted him, another viper flew crossways through the battle. Several laser bolts pelted the Sekaran lengthwise. The ship split into several large pieces, debris spinning away from Baifed.

"Woo-ieee!" came a shout over the comm. "You see that, Drin? You may win with a laser sword, but no one's a better pilot than I am." It was Jellal. Of course.

Drin wasn't in the mood for joviality. He had to see if Baifed had been gravely hurt. "Baifed, are you okay?" he asked.

No response came. The ship seemed dead in space as Drin approached with his viper. Did he lose power? There could still be hope. Drin could drop a cable and tow him back to the hangar bay. But if power had been completely removed, and there was a breach, Baifed could be dead in the cold of space, and he had no nanite armor to protect him.

Suddenly, thrust exhaust came from the port side of Baifed's viper. The ship began to move. "Brother Drin?" Baifed's voice came through the comm.

Drin exhaled. "Brother Baifed. Good to hear from you. Praise Yezuah."

"Praise Yezuah," Baifed said. "I had to reroute power. The blast must have taken out some of the main wiring. But it worked. All systems online. Let's make these heretics pay."

"I see an opening ahead. We can get to their main battleship," Jellal said. "Follow me."

They'd broken formation in the heat of battle, against Commander Shayne's orders, but it had to be done. Drin couldn't leave his brother to enemies in the cold of space.

They quickly regrouped. The three vipers formed a triangle, flying tightly together, with Jellal taking point at the top. The navigational computers locked in with one another. Commander Shayne veered his viper toward them, joining the formation and turning the squadron into a diamond shape.

"You thought you could do the attack run without your commander?" Shayne asked.

"Never dream of it," Jellal said.

The four vipers approached the hulking mass of the Sekaran battleship. They'd successfully made their way through the line of Sekaran fighters, and the ship loomed like a giant wall in front of them.

Point-defense laser-repeaters fired at them, causing them to have to break off. "Scramble," Commander Shayne said. "Target their shuttle bays first so the fighters can't launch reinforcements or return. These destroyers have their engines to the rear, so we'll loop around back and try to blast through. Let's go!"

Drin veered his viper away from the others. He dodged several laser bolts coming his way. The viper moved so quickly it blurred some of the features of the larger Sekaran ship, but Drin managed to target the open shuttle bays with the help of his AI. His bolts fired, and blasts covered where the bay doors would have been. It wasn't long before his viper whirled around the side of the ship for a longer run down the side of the rectangular vessel. Turrets popped out of the Sekaran ship, tracking and blasting laser fire toward him, but the viper was able to counter every move with amazing speed.

He targeted the various turrets, stationary on the ship, at least relative to Drin's movement. If he managed to take a few of those down, it would help with anyone else trying to attack the ship.

When he reached the rear of the vessel, he unloaded on the place where Commander Shayne had told him to fire. The shots didn't seem to do anything to the Sekaran ship other than to char its hull with laser blasts.

Baifed came up behind him. His shots blasted at the same place, and debris shot off the ship.

"Almost got it," Commander Shayne said. "We'll need to take another pass."

Sekaran fighters descended on them. They'd broken off from the main group in pursuit. Drin had one on his tail, Baifed had another. Drin couldn't see the others from his current location.

He tried to shake the fighter on him, slamming the controls left and right to act like he was going to be making more turns. The laser fire from the battleship slowed from the turrets they'd been able to take out already.

"I need some help here," Drin said. He hated saying it. Baifed and Jellal would never let him live it down, even if he'd helped them equally during the battle. But it was too dangerous to let his pride dictate the situation. Survival was paramount. If they failed here, the Sekarans would overrun Altequine, and all of their sacrifices—and the sacrifices of the Skree—would be for naught.

"Bank right," Jellal said through the comm.

"If I do that, I'll head right into their turret fire," Drin said.

"Dodge it. Trust me. It's the only way."

There couldn't be any delay. He was running out of maneuverable room between the fighters following him, more Sekarans up ahead, and the line of fire of the battleship's turrets. He had to trust his brother. In a quick maneuver, Drin banked right and hit his thrusters hard at the same time. If all went well, he would be able to pass through the turret fire in between bolts, but he had to time it perfectly.

Drin tensed, gripping hard on the viper's controls. Part of him wanted to shut his eyes, but doing so would be the deadliest thing he could do in the middle of space combat. Instead, he rode the thrusters through the enemy fire, ready for the life beyond. He'd done his duty to Yezuah, and he would be blessed in Heaven. Wouldn't he?

The moment wouldn't come, at least not for now. He passed through the enemy turret fire without an issue. The Sekaran fighter was still on his tail. It had banked with him, and it followed him directly into the turret fire.

The enemy disappeared on his tactical screen. Drin glanced over his shoulder, angling his ship upward to try to take a look and see what happened. All he could see was debris as the turrets recalibrated themselves to try to follow his ship. Drin sped out of the way, moving fast enough to keep from their aim.

"You see that?" Jellal chuckled. "Worked just like I said."

"It also could have killed me," Drin said.

"But the important part is...it didn't!"

Drin couldn't help but smile. The Lord's blessing was with them in this battle. How could he have even doubted?

"Drin," Commander Shayne said. "Your current vector puts you in a prime location for an attack run on the battleship's core. I'm transmitting coordinates. Lock your weapons on and head in. I'll be coming in on your three for a pincer attack."

Drin checked the tactical screen. The target illuminated. He programmed his weapons to lock in on the target. It was a small area, a chink in the armor. He would have to get close.

He banked his viper again, this time toward the enemy battleship. He would come in at an angle to ensure the turrets couldn't get an easy line on his ship. It would only take a few seconds to get there.

Out the side of the cockpit, Commander Shayne's Viper came up alongside him. They were almost there.

Turret fire blasted close to them, clipping Commander Shayne's ship on its wing. The viper destabilized and wobbled.

Drin pulled off to the side so he wouldn't risk getting hit. But they were too close to the target. He had to focus and hope Commander Shayne would regain control.

He fired his weapons. His lasers blasted at the ship, charring the Sekaran vessel's hull. Would the shots penetrate? He had no way of knowing. From beside him, Commander Shayne's blasts hit as well. He must have been able to keep his ship heading for the target.

Drin kept firing for as long as he could, heading straight for the ship. It would be cutting it close, but he couldn't see any signs as to whether his blasts were effective. He had to give it his all in this opening. As his viper came close to the Sekaran vessel, Drin held his breath. He pulled up on the controls, forcing the viper to make an extreme maneuver. The thrusters groaned in protest, and the gravitational force of the maneuver was too much for his artificial gravity to overcome. It was like a weight pressed down on his head. Harder, and even harder still. Drin found himself gasping for air.

The viper turned, narrowly missing a deadly collision with the Sekaran vessel. It sped along the hull of the Sekaran ship, the hull's features turning into a blurred gray from the speed of the run.

Drin pulled away. Gravity restored to normal. He could breathe again.

But he didn't see Commander Shayne's ship. Where had he gone?

He checked the area surrounding his cockpit, but it was only the blackness of space and the battle beyond. Before he could look at his tactical screen, Drin saw what happened to the Sekaran vessel.

The battleship lit up in brilliant glows of oranges and yellows. A million sparks going off at once. Its exterior portals collapsed in on themselves, and the ship seemed to crumple. Their attack run had struck true. The Sekarans were going to be down a capital ship. And with their work knocking out the shuttle bays, they wouldn't be able to dispatch more fighters.

Drin clenched a fist, proud of the victory. "We did it," he said to himself.

Commander Shayne's ship appeared in his vision. He'd doubled back behind the Sekaran vessel. "That was close!" Shayne said. "I lost stability and had to pull away from the ship so I didn't crash into it. It forced me to loop around the other side. Fortunately, their turret men were distracted from their ship imploding. We've done well. The battle's ours!"

The Templars cheered over the comm channel.

"We've gotta clean up the rest of the heretics. Let's send them back to Eltu!"

Drin turned around to complete the cleanup work. The Sekarans would know it was hopeless without their battleship. They wouldn't be any less dangerous, but the Elorians had the situation under control. Without a battleship, the Sekarans could do little real damage. Drin turned his viper toward the closest group of Sekaran fighters, and his brothers followed him.

# TEN

ANAIS HADN'T HAD MUCH TIME TO THUMB THROUGH THE Gospel of Marayh before the doctors pressed her back into service. After her work with the first Elorian, they wanted her healing capabilities back in action. Each instance proved equally taxing, even though the level of severity of the wounds she addressed diminished as time went on. After more than an hour of laying hands on various patients, Anais could barely stand. She found her balance becoming precarious, and she stumbled into a nearby bulkhead.

Vith attended to her, holding her upright. "Are you alright, child?"

"Yes, I just became a little dizzy for a moment," Anais said. Her left ear twitched, flopping across her forehead. Another sign she had taxed herself too much. "I think I need a rest."

One of the doctors hurried by. "You won't get one," he said. "The first wave of pilots is about to come back from the battle."

The battle? Anais had almost forgotten there was fighting going on outside the ship. The med bay had no exterior view, making it easy to forget recent events. Even if the ship were under assault, Anais didn't feel anything. It wasn't as if the blasts rocked her or the med bay, which meant the Sekaran attack hadn't been *too* successful, at least. And if the pilots were starting to come back in... "Is it over? Did we win?"

The doctor paused in front of a patient, but then looked back over his shoulder. "Reports I'm hearing is that we are victorious, yes."

Anais relaxed her shoulders, not having realized how much the worry of the battle had been grating on her. These last couple of days had been too much, bringing more stress on her even than when she had to engage in fighting at Altequine. Even her time as a slave to those awful Sekarans hadn't worn on her so much.

But everything was different now. The events all compounded upon each other. She was drained because her life kept spinning out of control, from one dangerous situation to another. It wasn't as if she'd had any preparation to handle this. She'd spent most of her time studying and partying, something she was sure she'd never do again. Her heart sank, missing her friends and family anew.

The pilots came into the med bay, interrupting her thoughts. Several Sekaran Templars and ordinary pilots made their way in to be treated for their wounds. One had the whole right side of his face charred, drooping and bloody. The nurses rushed him over to one of the biobeds.

Anais still hadn't recovered completely. She still felt a little dizzy, and her knees wobbled as if they would give way at any moment. All the same, she pushed herself to the tips of her toes to look above the others, in hopes she might see Drin. In truth, she hoped Drin wouldn't appear, because it would have meant he'd sustained injuries, but the hope he was alive—it meant far more to her than it should have.

As the pilots filtered in, Drin didn't come. Anais found herself disappointed, frowning.

"Too many injured is getting to you, child?" Vith asked. She maneuvered around the now crowded room with a deft ease coming from experience. She tended to the three wounded soldiers closest to Anais.

"No...it's just...I think I'm too tired."

"It's okay. You've done well. There's no life-threatening injuries here from what I can see. The Lord has blessed this group of pilots."

"Blessed us by vanquishing His enemies," one of the Elorian patients said.

"Indeed." Vith smiled at the man. "Stay still," she said to him as she wrapped an arm, which had a large gash in it. Once done with the task, she turned back to Anais. "Why don't you take a break, get out of the medical ward and relax, take a nap, or perhaps even read?"

Anais clutched the book Vith had given her. "It would be okay?"

"There's no shame in needing a break," Vith said. "Besides, I need to get back to work, and talking with you is slowing me down."

Anais nodded. The old Elorian nun moved on to another patient. If Anais was going to be allowed to leave, then she supposed she would. She stepped toward the exit doors, antici- pating one of the doctors would shout at her and demand she come back. None did.

As she entered the corridors of the ship, dozens of Elorians buzzed about. The mood was jovial among them. They joked, chatted, and playfully shoved each other as men were wont to do. The battle must have gone very well. She found their attitudes put her even more at ease.

Even though Vith had instructed her to rest, Anais found herself veering back toward the shuttle bay. If she could by chance find him easily on this massive vessel, her best bet would be there.

The first wave out had been the injured, followed by several of the technicians. The Templar pilots gathered together, talking in a circle. One of them held a rather large brown bottle which he passed around to the others. The whole group took swigs from the bottle as if it were the last drink they'd ever have.

Anais made her way through the shuttle bay, not wanting to intrude, but she also wanted to get a better look. She recognized a couple of the Elorians straight off. Baifed with his pointy and almost triangular beard, Jellal with a more boyish book and, finally, in the center of the group, was her ever stoic, brooding friend Drin. Her heart seemed to beat a little faster at the sight of him. She was thankful he made it out alive.

The Templars talked as she approached. Finally, one of them spotted her. Baifed. He narrowed his eyes. "The woman is here," he said.

Drin turned and met her eyes. "Anais," he said.

"Hey," Anais said, her heart fluttering. Fire filled her after the way he looked at her. It became too hot for her in her clothes. She shouldn't feel this way about Drin. It wouldn't go anywhere, but no matter how she tried, she found herself unable to stop the sensation. She bit down on her bottom lip.

Whether Drin sensed her awkwardness or not, she couldn't tell, but he broke with his companions, pushing past them to go to her. "What did you think of your first space battle?" he asked. The other Templars didn't watch them but resumed their conversations.

"I barely noticed it," Anais said, brushing her foot against the smooth, metallic floor. "We were so deep within the ship we couldn't really tell what was happening."

"Ah," Drin said. "I'm glad to know you were safe."

"Me too."

A moment passed. Drin looked back at the others, and then to her. He motioned to the book she had under her arm. "What's that?"

Anais brought the book into her hands and glanced down at it. "Something Sister Vith told me to read."

"If she says it's worth your reading, then I recommend you follow her advice. Her walk with the Lord is deep," Drin said.

Goosebumps formed on Anais' neck. It was as if some sort of spirit had overcome her. She couldn't quite place it. Could it be the nanites acting inside her? "I will," she said. "When I have a moment. I've been working on my healing while you were out, and I think I've found a way to control it. I helped the doctors."

"Good. We all have our gifts and our callings. You're on the path to finding yours."

The religious talk made her want to crawl inside a bulkhead and hide. She professed the Elorian faith as she promised Drin she would do. Their survival had been a miracle she couldn't deny. The nanites also were strange and powerful. But she couldn't be certain these stories about Yezuah were true or that it meant there was an all-powerful, single God. How could Drin be so sure? Her heart ached. She wanted what he had in many ways. Perhaps this was the right path. Only time would tell.

Anais moistened her lips. "I still don't feel like I belong here," she found herself saying.

Drin cocked his head at her, scrutinizing her. "I imagine as the only one of your people that would be the case. But with the nanites inside of you, you should remain under Elorian care."

He could see right through her. She missed her own people. More, the fact she didn't know what happened to her people grated on her. It was like a weight pressed on her shoulders, constricting her movement at all times. "Yeah. You're right. But I need to go back to my people." She met his eyes with as much confidence as she could muster. "Will you help me? Like you've helped the Skree?"

Drin frowned. For once, he shied away, his eyes darting to the floor in front of him. "I have to follow the orders of Father Cline and the Church."

"Talk to them again for me. Intercede for me," Anais said.

Someone laughed among the Templars. Anais caught a glimpse of one of them taking a very deep swig from the bottle and choking. The others seemed very amused. She wished she had a different setting for their talk.

"I'll do it," Drin said finally. He lifted his chin. "Let's go find Father Cline."

"Now?" Anais blinked.

"Now." Without another word, Drin turned to leave the shuttle bay. His other Templars called back for him, but he moved like a man on a mission.

Anais scurried to catch up with him as they returned to the chapel, and to Father Cline. The priest was already at his desk in his office this time, reviewing the action of the latest battle and taking copious notes as to the tactics of both his men and the enemy.

Father Cline furrowed his brow as he watched the scene in front of him. "I see Templar Baifed became somewhat aggressive and broke with the line. We need to stick together as a cohesive unit."

"We did our best under the circumstances," Drin said.

Father Cline motioned to flick the image off, turning toward Drin and Anais. "So you did. And you were victorious, which is what matters." He paused. "You've come to ask for assistance with the girl."

Anais stiffened at being called *the girl*.

"I have," Drin said, lifting his chin.

"No need to posture, Templar Drin. I've been expecting it. I've told her we cannot dispatch the Templars to her homeworld without deliberation from the Church, and that fact remains the case even now."

"But—" Anais started.

Drin held up a hand. "Patience."

Father Cline's lips ticked upward into a wry smile. "The more you observe and go with God, the more you can look through the eyes of another and understand."

He folded his hands on his desk and leaned toward them. "This trip to Konsin II was not supposed to happen either. Drin was never intended to go here. He should have stayed with the vessel and never pursued his journey. That same journey brought him closer to God and freed a world from Sekaran occupation. It had to have been God's plan, despite what the Church had in mind. We are fallible, after all."

"Does that mean you're going to go?"

"Me?" Father Cline chuckled. "No. It is not my place, nor the place of the *Justicar*. But you have seen with your own eyes the miracles of Yezuah, and how one of the faithful can change the course of an entire world, have you not?"

"Father Cline, I—" Drin interrupted.

This time, Father Cline held up a hand. "Ah, ah! Patience," he repeated, with a little glint in his eyes. "I know you have just returned to this family of believers, Drin, and that you wish to be among us and further your fellowship. However, you are very adamant in helping this girl to the point where I see you would give up your life for her as soon as you would for one of your brothers. I'm hoping you've stayed true to your vows."

"I have been chaste," Drin said.

Father Cline nodded. "Then there is no harm in sending you to escort her, to obtain information on behalf of the Holy Church. I would not wish for you to leave the fraternity of your brothers again, however. You may be escorted by another Templar. Is there one in whom you would choose?"

"Jellal," Drin said. He barely moved when he spoke, focused forward.

"Then it will be so. Once we are done retrieving the salvage and information from this battle, you and Jellal will take one of the transports with the girl here, and her companion. What was her name?"

"Lyssa," Anais said. She could barely believe this was happening. Everything had gone so fast during the battles these last couple of days. Her healing abilities. Drin's move to help her. And now she was going to be able to go home! She could hardly believe it. Butterflies trickled up her stomach and into her chest.

"She'll return with you. Should that suffice?" Father Cline asked.

"Yes. Better than suffice. Thank you!" Lyssa said.

Someone came into the office behind them. Lyssa turned. The Skree, Err-dio, stood in the doorway, his multiple hands crossed over his chest. "Father Cline. I've meant to introduce myself to you. I am Err-dio, warrior of the Skree. I owe my life to Templar Drin multiple times over, and I wish to be pressed into service as his squire. Where he goes, I will follow and assist to the best of my abilities for as long as I live, so help me God."

Father Cline raised a brow. "That is a strong oath. Your faith guides you, I can see."

Err-dio nodded.

"This could be dangerous," Drin said.

"No more dangerous than our last battles have been," Err-dio said. "I read your Holy Book. It says the tribulations I endure in service of our Lord will be repaid to me tenfold in heaven. Is this not true?"

"It is," Drin said.

"Then I see no reason to worry."

Anais wished she had that kind of faith. She found herself blushing out of embarrassment. But nothing could spoil the moment. She would be able to go home, and she had a group of people to help her make sure Pyus would be safe and free from

Sekarans. She clasped her hands together. "Great. When do we leave?"

"As soon as we find Jellal and fix his nanites like you did for me. We might want to show one of the other healers how to do it as well. Come on," Drin said, motioning for her to follow.

# ELEVEN

Parthenon Station hung in space, a giant cylinder, rotating to provide its own gravity. Thousands of tiny lights shone, making it a beacon. As their shuttle came closer, Drin could see the sheer magnitude of the space station, it turning into an endless wall in front of them as the shuttle made its way toward the docking bay.

A docking bay would be more accurate, as the station had dozens of them. It was a commerce hub, with more ships coming in and out than there were docking slots. They had to pause and wait while a ship in front of them landed in the bay and unloaded. Once the passengers inside were out, the station dock master dropped a forcefield to decompress the bay.

Jellal piloted the ship with Drin as co-pilot while Err-dio stayed in the back with the two women. A co-pilot in this instance had little to do other than to wait while the station's tractor beams grabbed a hold of the shuttle and brought it into its resting place. Once docked, the lights in the bay flashed from red to green to let the shuttle passengers know it was safe to exit the ship. Several technicians entered the bay, loading and unloading cargo from several of the other shuttles docked in the facility.

Drin popped the hatch. The pressure shifted to station normal, and the five travelers departed the ship. The shuttle bay was filled with a mix of all sorts of races, peoples Drin had never seen before. Many of the stationers had a gray hue to their skins, with a slick, shiny quality to them, and a giant sharp point atop their heads. They chattered in a strange language Drin didn't understand.

"We need to find Nagell," Anais said.

"Do you have any other contact than a name? This station holds more than three hundred thousand inhabitants at any given time," Jellal said.

One of the local beings approached. "Do you need assistance moving bags to your lodgings?" he asked.

"We're not certain how long we'll be staying," Drin said.

"Do you know where to find Nagell?" asked Lyssa, the other Pyus girl. Drin hadn't spoken much to her. She seemed timider than Anais in interacting with strangers.

"Nagell? The chief executive?" the creature sounded amused.

"That's him," Anais said.

"This is the lower level docking bay. He's in the command center."

"Can you lead us to him?" Drin asked.

The creature laughed. "If I could, we wouldn't be in the lower levels." He shook its head and wobbled away from them. As he walked away, his long, flat feet pattered on the floor.

Drin crossed his arms. "He didn't seem particularly friendly. I thought you said this Nagell worked with your father?" Drin asked.

Anais' left ear twitched. "He did, but it's not like we announced we were coming."

"How did you contact him before?" Drin asked.

"Through the comm," Anais said.

The staff hurried, rushing out of the bay. The lighting flashed red again, and an audible alarm sounded. "Warning, decompression in five minutes. Shuttle docking. Please vacate the docking bay," a loud voice said.

"We should go," Jellal said. "We'll have to get our stuff later."

Drin and the others hurried out of the shuttle bay. An alarm blared as they crossed the threshold into the station hallway. People crowded around them, creating an environment of mass confusion. Anais clung to Drin, gripping onto his wrist. He tensed his arm instinctively but found a strange comfort in having her rely on him.

Anais padded beside him as they weaved through people. "I wonder how long until we'll be able to get back in," she asked.

"Hours," a passerby said before Drin could turn. "They're recompressing the bay with a methane atmosphere."

Drin frowned as he led Anais and the others to an area they could gather around without getting run over. "This station has a feel to it, it's hard to explain. Chaotic."

"Agreed," Jellal said. "This is what happens when the secular take over."

Lyssa crossed her arms. "Pyus is secular. It's not like this. We just came at a bad time," she said.

Anais leaned against the metal wall. "We can sit and complain all we want, but we're stuck out here. Should we rent a place?"

"I'm not sure any of us have the funds to do so," Drin said, watching Anais. "The Templar life is one which renounces material goods and money."

Anais slumped her shoulders, a dejected frown crossing her face.

Seeing her in such a state tugged at Drin's heart. He had his vows to the church, but even with those, it was hard to deny that he cared for Anais. They had erred in coming to the station. Father

Cline had given them warnings about leaving without the church's deliberations, but they had been insistent and hurried away from the *Justicar* without planning. It was stupid in hindsight. None of them had any experience outside their own people. None of them had any resources. Perhaps it was a lesson Father Cline had meant to teach them.

"We have to find the station CEO. He talked to us before," Anais said under her breath.

"Yes," Drin said, crossing his arms. "But how?"

"We'll have to talk our way into it," Lyssa said.

Anais turned to the other Pyus woman. They looked alike in some ways, though Lyssa had an amber hue to her fur where Anais was pure white like when the sunlight reflected across fresh snow. Drin shook his head. He couldn't be thinking such thoughts. He would have to confess his sins as soon as he had a chance.

"How?" Anais asked.

"We're daughters of merchant lords," Lyssa said. "We'll negotiate."

"We don't have anything to negotiate with," Anais said.

Lyssa veered back down the long corridor. "They don't have to know that. Come on," she said.

Drin followed her. The fool girl was running off again without much of a plan. The first instance hadn't been her fault, but Drin was beginning to wonder if Pyus had a propensity toward flightiness as a species.

He didn't voice his opinion. Nor did Jellal or Err-dio. They all followed Lyssa as she moved with a small crowd of people to a large open area with a domed ceiling. The ceiling had different windows looking down upon them, a giant open market bigger than the city of Altequine, but all contained. Thousands of people talked at once. Soft music played from hidden speakers. The domed panels had a soft red hue as if they were receiving light from a red giant. Small hovering platforms lifted people above the crowd to different shops.

Some of the shops were open—food carts, laser art body modification, and other artistic endeavors in view—while others were in smaller, contained rooms. Still others were completely blacked out in the windows with no advertisements or discernible signs. An armed guard with a long laser-rifle stood in front of one of them. Weapons wouldn't be banned here, at the very least. The guard didn't seem to be wearing a security uniform.

Lyssa made straight for the guard.

Drin grabbed her by the wrist to stop her. "What do you think you're doing?"

"Yeah," Anais said. "I can't say he looks inviting."

"I figure if he's allowed such an open display, he must be representing someone important. Someone important here is probably close with the station CEO. We'll see," Lyssa said. She continued toward the guard. She stopped just in front of the armored man, standing nearly a full head of height beneath him, and that was with her long, erect ears.

"What do you want?" the man asked through a voice modulator. The eye slots in his helmet were dark, reflecting Lyssa's face in them.

"Who's inside?" Lyssa asked in a cheerful tone.

"None of your business."

"We're very important dignitaries from Pyus, and we need to get a hold of the station CEO Nagell. Please...there could be contracts in it later. You do guard work for hire, yes?"

The man shifted. "I do."

"Couldn't you tell whoever's inside there are important people who could be useful for business, and we want a brief meeting?"

The guard looked behind him. "I suppose I could tell him someone's at the door."

"Thanks," Lyssa said, stepping back. She shot a smug glance to Drin and Anais.

Drin narrowed his eyes, still unsure. The whole conversation seemed preposterous to him. If he were guarding this shop...

The guard pressed his hand to the lock, trigging the shop's door mechanism to open. The door rolled to the side, a circular entrance. He disappeared inside. For several moments, Drin and his companions waited, several shoppers passing by, none sparing more than a glance for the party. Business as usual on a busy station.

A stalk-like bug creature appeared from inside, the guard following close behind. The creature took one look at the party with its beady eyes. "Elorians!" he shrieked. "Kill them!"

Jellal and Drin glanced at each other. This was unexpected. They barely had time to erect their shields before the guard opened fire with his rifle.

These laser blasts were of a tighter concentration than the base Sekaran laser-repeaters. Drin felt the force of it causing him to slide backward on the slick floors of the station. The pink field surrounded him, holding steady. He formed a laser sword in his hand. Jellal followed suit.

"There must be some kind of mistake," Lyssa pleaded, backpedaling. "We just wanted to talk."

"We don't talk with zealots!" the bug creature shouted. It produced its own laser-repeater.

Err-dio rushed forward and tackled the bug-creature. The frontal attack caught the creature off guard, and he fell to the ground, dropping his weapon in the process. His guard wasn't so careless. He fired two shots, one at Jellal, one at Drin, forcing them backward and off balance. Their shields would hold through the fire, but not for many shots longer. They had to take him down quickly.

Before Drin could recover his balance and push forward,

several other guards flooded from around the corner. These looked more official than the one defending the bug-creature. They all had a circular logo with a three-pronged symbol in the middle of it. Drin had seen that logo elsewhere on the station. They'd drawn station security.

"Hands up!" one of the station guards said. "Everyone. No violence on the commerce floor."

Drin watched his enemy intently, not about to drop his shields and risk injury while his opponent still had his rifle pointed at him. The man lowered his rifle. Station security swarmed him, Drin, and Jellal. Drin let his light sword dissipate and dropped his shielding. The guards pointed their weapons at him, all too close.

"You're going to have to come into detention for a statement at the very least. We'll see if it warrants pressing charges," one of the station guards said.

"We don't want any trouble," Drin said.

Another creature made its way through the crowd of security, pushing them to the side. "What's going on here?" The creature was much shorter than the others, with long eyes and a stubby, moist nose that reflected light. It was a furred creature like Anais, but different in many ways. It had whiskers.

"That's Nagell," Anais said to Drin. She brushed past him and stood before the smaller creature. "Nagell! It's me. Anais."

The shorter creature sniffed at the air in front of Anais and stepped back to observe her. "In the flesh? But why are you here?" He turned to face Drin, his countenance appearing none too friendly. "And what are you doing with the religious crazies?"

"They're not crazy..." Anais said, biting on her lower lip. "Would you mind letting them go, though?"

Nagell motioned to the guards. They lowered their guns in turn. "Let's adjourn to a more private location and you can tell me what's going on. I would never have expected to see you and *them* together, my dear Carver."

Anais nodded and motioned to the others. "Come on."

Drin followed, keeping quiet. He had to be vigilant and wary. Anti-Elorian prejudice was not uncommon throughout the galaxy, especially where Sekarans were involved, but in free areas driven by commerce, Drin had never seen such animosity. Of course, he'd had the full might of the Templars at his back whenever he'd interacted with other species in the galaxy. Someone had to be vigilant here, however. He glanced to Jellal and Err-dio. Both of the men seemed nearly as cautious as he was. Err-dio nodded to him in understanding.

They crossed through the big commerce dome and into one of the doors along the side. The doors shut, and Nagell scanned his handprint. The small chamber lifted into the air at immense speeds, and stopped at top level, where the doors opened again into a large conference room.

The place exemplified industry—large windows overlooking the commerce level below, a table in the middle mode of dark wood, a holoprojector, and several paintings of Nagell's species in gray, formal business attire. "Welcome to my executive conference room," Nagell said. He motioned for the guards to wait outside, leaving him alone with the five of them. "Please, make yourselves comfortable."

Drin moved to a chair near side of the table. Jellal leaned back against the wall, crossing his arms. "I'll stand. It's been a long ride in the pilot's chair," Jellal said.

"Whatever suits you," Nagell said, seating himself.

The two Pyus girls sat on Nagell's side of the table, and Err-dio moved next to Drin.

"We're trying to get information on the planet Pyus," Drin began.

Nagell held a hand up. "Let's start at the beginning. Ms. Carver, why are you here with these Elorians...and someone from a species I've never seen before?" He motioned to them as if they were mere objects.

Lyssa titled her head. "They're my friends. Drin saved me when the Sekarans kidnapped me, and he saved my life more times after that. He and Jellal are here to help."

Nagell peered at Drin for a long while. "Elorians are dangerous, Ms. Carver. As much or more so than the Sekarans."

"Heresy," Jellal said.

The room fell into tense silence. Drin kept his face as stoic as possible, but he could feel Jellal seething from behind him. "Insults are not going to get us anywhere," Drin said.

"No, I suppose they're not." Nagell leaned back into his chair. "Your companions are who you choose, but forgive me if it causes me and others on the station here a little bit of trepidation. Many of us have experienced the fallout of their war with the Sekarans, and we want to be as far away from it as possible."

"Understandable," Anais said. "Regardless, they've volunteered to help me return to Pyus and assist my people."

"If the Sekarans have sacked your world, the five of you won't make a dent," Nagell said.

"I know. That's why we're here," Anais said. She glanced to Lyssa and back to him again. "We need your help."

Nagell shook his head. "I'm not some revolutionary. I have a station to run, and involving ourselves in a conflict with the Sekarans is a surefire way to get them to pay too much attention to us. They might end up blowing this place into bits. We can't. We really can.t"

"There has to be someone who will help."

"You could always try one of the mercenary guilds," Nagell aid. "But they know exactly how deadly this conflict between your friends..." he motioned to Drin and Jellal, "and the Sekarans can be. They're not a charity, and they don't make money by getting into prolonged conflicts where they lose a lot of men."

"We don't have any money," Lyssa said, frowning. "I mean, we could, but we'd probably have to go to Pyus first and see what we could gather up."

"If you do that, we'll likely get captured or worse," Drin said. "No, we need to ascertain exactly how large the Sekaran force is first before we descend on your planet."

Nagell clicked his tongue. "I may be able to assist you in your financial problem." He flicked the holoprojector on and entered some information into his keyboard. Data came up on the stream, and finally information listing numbers in the thousands.

"What's that?" Lyssa asked.

"Credits," Nagell said. "We did business with the Carver Merchant Lord Family on Pyus, as you are aware. Since your world was taken, we couldn't make the transfer from the last shipment of craft goods. They've been sitting in an account—accruing interest—for months now."

Anais' jaw nearly hit the floor. "Eighty million credits? That's a lot of money."

"Enough to buy several of your own ships and outfit them with weaponry," Nagell said.

"Or to add to the coffers of the Holy Church," Jellal said from the wall.

"We have a mission, Jellal," Drin said. Sometimes the other Templars were too focused on what the church could use. If they freed a world from Sekaran rule, though, how much more benefit could it be to the galaxy and the reputation of the church among it?

"Yes," Anais said coolly. "We're here for one reason. Ships won't do us good either. What were you saying about mercenaries?"

The shorter creature waved her suggestion off. "Just words. Ones I probably shouldn't have uttered. You're very innocent, I can tell," Nagell said. "If you want to forget about this whole business and come work for us here, I can also tell you're a very diligent worker with a shrewd mind. We can use you. Your friends might even be useful in security."

"No," Lyssa said. "We're going to liberate our world."

Nagell sighed. "Suit yourselves. If you want to get involved with mercenaries, do so at your own risk. They're only loyal to one thing. If you run out of credits, you'll find you'll run out of friends quickly."

"Not if we convert them," Jellal said.

Nagell laughed. His large eyes twinkled at Drin. "I don't think your friend intends to be funny, but he very much is."

Drin grunted.

"Anyway," Nagell said. "I have friends among the Sagitar mercenary guild. We've hired them in the past. You can tell them I sent you. Their fleet is currently recuperating in the Cinzi sector. I can get you your credits and send you on your way with some food and supplies, but that's the best I can do."

Anais stood, pressing her hands on the table. The room didn't feel like they've achieved any sort of victory—in fact, quite the opposite. Drin was skeptical about these mercenaries. By Jellal's body language, he downright hated them. Moreover, why should they trust this Nagell? On the other hand, he'd allowed them their freedom after security had captured them, and apparently honored his debts. It was about all one could ask from an infidel.

"Let's get going," Anais said. "Every minute we waste is another minute people in Pyus could be dying...or worse." Her eyes darkened as she said those last words, and it looked like the fur stood on her arms.

Drin watched her carefully. He wanted to help direct matters, but she was so determined, and this was a better start than he could have anticipated. All he could do was pray to the Lord this would be the proper path.

# TWELVE

Anais smiled to herself. The shuttle travelled through hyperspace, the stars blurring before them into brilliant light. This had gone far better than she'd expected.

Nagell had really done right by her family. She couldn't believe how many credits he let them walk out of the station with —and he didn't even charge them docking or refueling fees. All was looking up for her world. Was this why Drin lectured her about trusting in God? He kept telling her everything would work out in the end if she kept the faith. Maybe he had something to his intense devotion to religion.

She thought of the book Vith had given her, detailing the lives of women in the Elorian religion. Anais had been too excited with the prospect of going home to read them thus far. Her mind whirled, imagining meeting with the mercenary captain, hiring them and the fleet and descending on Pyus, chasing off those terrible Sekarans. With Drin and Jellal, it would have to go much like the battle of Altequine did. The two of them could probably secure a whole planet by themselves. Nothing could go wrong. Soon, she would be home, and everything would return to normal.

If her family had survived. Anais cast her eyes aside, not wanting to think those negative thoughts.

"Everything okay?" Lyssa asked.

"Yeah. Just nervous, I guess."

"Me too," Lyssa said. "I hope everyone back home is okay."

"Yeah."

The hum of the ship's engines stopped the shuttle from descending into pure silence. Jellal tapped on the piloting controls. "We're about to drop out of hyperspace," he said.

The cockpit window shifted from bright light to the blackness of space, with stars becoming small dots illuminating the void's backdrop once more. They didn't feel the ship's gravitational dampeners, but the open space made for a stark contrast.

"I don't see any planets or stars here."

"It's just a sector of space," Jellal said. "Between stars. A good hiding spot, tactically."

"Indeed," Drin said. "Any ships on your scanners?"

Jellal brought up the tactical display. "Not that I see. Let me push their range." He hit the controls again. Several blips appeared at the edge of the display. "Not sure if those are asteroids or ships, but I suppose we'll find out."

"Broadcast a message that we're friendlies not looking for a battle," Drin said.

"Good idea. We don't want them to be jumpy." Jellal sent the message.

They drifted closer to the blips on the screen. Anais's heart fluttered. This would be it, their best chance to get a fleet to Pyus. They approached what appeared to be a substantive fleet of ships. The ships were painted in blues and golds, apparently the colors to signify the Sagitars. It was a nice change to look at from the unpainted, functional war vessels of the Elorians. These ships were well lit, with several of their lights blasting into deep space. Smaller ships, drones, and bots surrounded the larger vessels, some working and repairing the hulls. It was a busy scene. Which ship was the lead vessel, and who would they talk to?

"We're getting a comm on frequency zeta," Jellal said.

"Visual?" Drin asked.

Jellal nodded.

"Bring it up."

The cockpit window shimmered into another new scene, one of a battle bridge behind them. A creature with several spiky horns protruding from his face, blood red eyes, and skin painted in intense colors that matched the hulls of their ship appeared. "Who are you, and how did you find us?"

Anais opened her mouth, but Drin held up a hand.

"My name is Drin, Templar of the *Justicar*. My companions and I come seeking your fleet's aid. Please hear us out."

The spiked creature leaned toward them, scrutinizing. "Templar? Elorian?"

Drin's chin rose proudly. "I am."

"Cut your engines. Our tractor beam will pull you in," the spiked man said. His image cut out, and the view returned to the fleet in front of them.

Jellal hit the controls to turn off the engines, and they waited.

Tractor beams were somewhat of a misnomer, more of a gravitational pull than any sort of laser beam. It couldn't be seen from the shuttle's cockpit, but the fleet's beam had gripped them and pulled the shuttle in toward the largest of the ships.

The ship eclipsed the view of anything else, and as they came closer, Anais could see a small cargo bay they were being pulled into. It didn't look like the Elorian's fleet bay, but one more meant for storage. They must not receive many visitors on the mercenary vessel.

The bay compressed and Drin opened the ramp. He took the lead with Anais close behind, and then the others, but he stopped suddenly when he reached the bottom. Anais nearly slammed into him. "Drin, what are you—"

She received her answer when she looked past him. More than twenty armored mercenaries had weapons trained right on them. Lyssa gasped from behind Anais.

"What's going on?" Drin asked.

"You're going to the brig," one of the armored mercenaries said. He motioned his rifle. "No funny business."

Drin kept his hands up and moved forward in the direction the mercenary had pointed. Anais followed, not wanting to get separated from him and seeing no good direction to run away from their captors. What was going on here? Nagell made it sound as if these mercenaries would be amicable to them. This looked anything but friendly.

"Keep moving," the merc said.

They pressed forward while other mercs led the way through the ship. The different sections were color-coded, but Anais couldn't tell what they represented. Eventually, they made their way to an area with a forcefield. One of the mercs dropped the field. Another pushed Anais in the back with his gun, forcing her to stumble forward into a small cell. Her companions followed.

When she turned, the forcefield had been re-erected, a translucent red light that flickered. The field would shock anyone who attempted to touch it. "We didn't do anything," Anais protested.

"You brought Elorians to our base," the merc said. He motioned to his men, and they marched back down the hall. He didn't stop to chat any further, leaving them in the cell.

Anais couldn't help but bring her hand close to the forcefield. How did this happen? They shouldn't be stuck in here. Everything was going so well. Did the rest of the galaxy really hate her newfound friends this much?

Drin grabbed her by the wrist. "Be careful about touching that. The shock can be deadly."

"It's not that bad," Jellal said.

Err-dio stepped toward the flickering light. "I wonder what it would take to short it out.

Drin released Anais' hand and paced the length of the cell. "It's possible Jellal and I could use our nanites to break our way out of here, but we don't know the layout of the ship, or what we'd be up against."

"We can try talking to them," Lyssa said.

"They don't seem to want to talk with *our* kind," Jellal said.

Anais turned toward them, crossing her arms over her chest. "Why do so many people hate Elorians anyway?"

Jellal and Drin looked at each other.

"Their souls have been corrupted," Jellal said.

Drin sighed. "It's for the same reason I nearly left the Templars. The burden became too much for me. Everywhere we go, there is death, destruction. It's because we're fighting against the Sekarans, but it feels like it's never-ending. Sometimes, whole worlds are destroyed in our wake. We do our best to rebuild, but..." He lowered his head.

"Sometimes our efforts aren't enough. Especially for those who flee their worlds and don't return to see the good we do," Jellal said.

"I think the church needs to do more to be ambassadors toward the public. If they spent some time doing that, it would solve a lot of these perception problems," Drin said.

"Maybe that's what I can do. Once we're done," Anais said. It didn't sound like a bad plan. She hadn't considered what her purpose would be after she rescued her people on Pyus—if she managed to accomplish the task. She could hardly go back to school. It'd be possible to get involved in trading through her father's empire with the merchant lords, but that didn't appeal to her. Helping the galaxy, bringing peace, and a good message. She could see herself in such a position.

They had to make it out of here, first.

"That's all fine and good talk," Lyssa said. "But in case you hadn't noticed, we're stuck in a cell and no one seems to be coming to talk to us about what they intend to do with us, let alone offer us a way out."

"This is true," Drin said. He nodded to Jellal and sat on the floor with his legs crossed underneath him. Jellal did the same. They both placed their hands on their knees.

"What are you doing?" Anais.

Drin looked up at her. If she didn't know better, she would have thought he was amused with her. "We're going to meditate and pray on our situation."

"God will show us a way," Jellal agreed.

Both men closed their eyes. Err-dio tepidly sat next to them in the same posture.

Anais met Lyssa's eyes and shook her head. She had some faith in the Elorian religion, but they could take it to extremes. She just wanted to escape sooner rather than later. Every moment they stayed here was another moment the Sekarans wreaked havoc on her world.

# THIRTEEN

"DRIN. DRIN! WAKE UP."

The voice sounded muffled at first, but as Drin returned to alertness, he could hear Anais speaking. He opened his eyes slowly, allowing them to adjust to the light. How long had he been asleep? The last thing he recalled was meditating and praying, and Jellal doing the same. A quick glance to his side revealed his Templar brother awake and grinning. Jellal motioned his head to the front of the cell.

When his eyes adjusted, Drin saw a large man with pink skin, wearing what looked to be a black uniform. The uniform had gemstones on it which appeared to denote rank. Two guards carrying very large rifles flanked each side of him. The man had to be someone important.

"Are you going to rise to speak with me, prisoners?" the man asked.

Anais and Lyssa were already on their feet, as was Err-dio. Only Jellal and Drin remained on the floor. While Drin considered rebelling, if only to irk the man, from his current position, it wouldn't do his group any good. He stood, and Jellal followed his lead.

"Better. I heard Elorians wouldn't obey any authority outside of their God. It's interesting to hear some rumors are false."

Drin remained quiet as the man surveyed them.

"Are you an officer on this ship?" Lyssa asked. "We've come from Parthenon Station. We're friends of Nagell."

The man's mouth up-ticked into a grin. "Nagell? I haven't seen him in ages. Why would Nagell be hanging around Elorians? Doesn't he know they bring destruction wherever they go?"

Drin didn't need to look back at Jellal to know his companion was seething. He just hoped Jellal could hold it in. The man was testing them, and they had to play by his rules for now.

"Our friends rescued us. It's a long story. Maybe we could tell it...somewhere less cramped?" Lyssa asked.

Drin had to admit the other Pyus girl had a way of talking out of situations. Anais' eyes glimmered with pride in her friend. Drin still remained quiet. Sometimes, wisdom meant knowing when not to speak nor act.

"I like your gumption," the man said. He motioned to the guards and turned. "Follow me."

The guards flanked him and left the forcefield down. Drin looked at the others but took a step forward. His friends moved with him. The man seemed to want to talk to Lyssa, and so he waited for her to catch up with him so she could walk beside him.

"I'm Admiral Domen, leader of the Sagitar fleet," the man said as they wound through several corridors. Officers and soldiers passed them, paying heed to Domen but ignoring the prisoners. The ship was huge, and Drin had no sense of his location within the vessel. "Tell me your story."

Lyssa recounted the battles on Konsin II, giving a very generous account of how the Elorians liberated the Skree people. Err-dio confirmed her words, drawing a raised brow from Domen.

"You were enslaved on a desert planet with few resources, no wonder I'd never seen your kind before," Domen said. "You look like you'd be good workers."

"The Sekarans had many of us performing technical mainte-nance on their vehicles and war machines," he said.

"There may be room for some of your kind in my fleet," Domen said. "Let them know...assuming I let you leave here."

"I will," Err-dio said.

Lyssa continued with her tale up until the point they reached Parthenon Station. "You see, the Sekarans invaded our world as well. And we're at a loss as to what to do. We need to see just how overwhelmed Pyus is and formulate a plan to do something."

Domen stopped at a door. One of his guards opened it for him. It opened into a small, holographic lounge with chairs facing a realistic display of an ocean. A red sun hung in the sky, making the atmosphere a blood-orange coloration. If Drin didn't know he were in a ship, he wouldn't be able to tell it from an actual beach. It felt like he'd been transported to another world, especially when the door closed behind him.

"This is my office," Domen said. "Or rather, where I entertain guests. I like to relax here. What you're seeing now is a scene from my homeworld. That is...my homeworld before the Elorians and Sekarans battled over the system and made the planet uninhabit-able. The fallout from the nuclear explosions isn't quite as nice as this view." He cast his eyes on Drin.

Drin held firm. It wasn't as if he had bombed the man's home-world. And he didn't know the specifics of what had transpired, but the account did cause his heart to sink in his chest. Drin had run from the Elorian fleet when the violence became too over-whelming for him. It was true that the war with the Sekarans had brought about horrors for many, and it never seemed to end. He struggled with this as part of his faith. He longed for Yezuah to return and bring peace to the galaxy.

"Please, have seats," Domen said. He took one chair for his

own. He didn't seem to want to make the Elorians present pay for the war crimes, but he wasn't afraid to mention them either.

Fortunately, Jellal appeared to be of the same mind as Drin. Nothing good would happen by arguing here, and they seemed to be making progress with Lyssa speaking.

"Thank you," Lyssa said. Anais took the chair next to her.

"If I understand your situation," Domen said, relaxing back into his chair, "you want the help of the Sagitar for at least a recon mission of your world. We are not the most inexpensive fleet in the galaxy. Our reputations span the spiral arm, and we're very choosy about contracts we take. Not many would be happy to take ones where Sekarans and Elorians are involved."

"But it's our world. We can pay. Nagell said we had enough funds to be able to buy our own small fleet."

Domen raised a brow. "Oh? You have my attention."

"Whatever it takes, we'll make it happen," Anais said. "And if we liberate our world, you'll have the thanks of all of the merchant lords. We'll be able to reward you handsomely."

"How much are we talking about?"

Anais opened her mouth to speak, but Lyssa glared at her, and she closed it again.

Drin tried not to let his amusement cross his face. Lyssa knew how to negotiate. Anais was still green. She had a pure heart, though. Drin had become accustomed to her habits, her rushing into situations head-first. He found them to be endearing traits.

"Eight thousand credits," Lyssa said.

Her voice sounded harder than usual. Negotiating, Drin realized. These were people descended from merchant lords. They probably had a better handle on how to deal with a mercenary than he did. The Templars had been trained to despise mercenaries. After all, someone fighting for money couldn't also be serving God as master.

Domen laughed. "That might get you one ship, and for a

limited time at that. There'll be hazard pay going into any situation with Sekarans to account for. I applaud your attempts at negotiation." He narrowed his eyes at Lyssa. "If you had three times that amount at your disposal, perhaps we could initiate a contract, but at that level, I should probably send you on your way." He moved to stand back up.

"Wait," Lyssa said.

Domen paused, giving her a wry smile. "Yes?"

"We can probably get you twenty thousand credits, though we'll have to talk the terms of what you're providing," Lyssa said.

"An escort. Transport?" Domen asked.

Lyssa shook her head. "More than that. I..." She glanced to Drin. "My companions here can discuss the logistics."

"The tactical situation is unknown," Drin said without missing a beat. "The Sekarans could have a warship in the system, a whole fleet, or they could have left a small retention force on the planet."

"So, you'll need some reconnaissance work done." Domen folded his hands together.

"We can do most of the work ourselves," Drin said. "But we might need some back up in case we run into trouble."

"Hmm," Domen said. "Unknown danger quantity. We can agree on twenty thousand, but if there's hazard pay in terms of prolonged space combat with a capital warship, we will want to collect an extra twenty-five percent, and to include a recon team escort—let's say four soldiers—that will cost you an extra five thousand credits per standard week."

"Deal."

"Deal?" Drin cocked his head. "We don't need their soldiers at that price."

"We might," Lyssa said, looking to him. She turned her attention back to Domen. "If we do need you for battle after we assess the situation. What then?"

"Then we'll see what you can come up with for more funds.

Combat on a planetary scale can take a lot of time, and be very costly."

Drin had full awareness of this. He'd invaded several planets with the Templars. Some they'd had to bomb and bring down most of the infrastructure just to get a foothold.

Altequine had been all too easy to subdue, and it was only because the Sekarans didn't leave much of a force behind. The desert world didn't hold much value to them because of its location and because of its limited resources. Pyus might be different. Drin hadn't been there, but given the spoiled lifestyles the women seemed to lead, he could only imagine it'd be a more valuable planet to hold.

Even with the help of mercenaries, they would need to be careful. "We need to have a plan. Worst case contingencies, best case scenarios. Even with a fleet this size, we don't want to fall prey to any Sekaran traps."

Domen stood finally. "Indeed we do. I'm going to call in two strategists to assist you in the planning phase. One for the ground assault and one for our space tactics. That is...if your funds clear."

"They will," Lyssa said.

"I believe you. We'll handle the accounting and meet in the war room in three hours. My guards will see you to guest quarters. We wouldn't want paying customers to be locked up in a cell."

They shouldn't have been in a cell to begin with, but Drin wasn't about to argue with the better accommodations or spoil the good fortune they'd found. Still, the mercenaries seemed all too casual about this, as did Lyssa and Anais. They didn't comprehend the true threat the Sekarans could pose, even from their bad experiences with the infidels.

Jellal understood. He moved closer to Drin when Domen made his way to the door. The hologram of the beach melted into the entrance doorway, and the doors reopened. Domen barked orders to his guards. "I don't like this," Jellal said. "We should contact Father Cline and ask him for reinforcements."

"Father Cline was already very generous with us," Drin said. "We'll make do with what we must, but we should inform the church of what we're doing and what our plans are. I have a feeling we'll need them ready to mobilize in the future."

Jellal nodded. "I'll prepare a report and a transmission to the *Justicar*."

"Good," Drin said.

Anais came up beside him, smiling wider than he'd seen her do before. She was so full of hope—she looked beautiful. Her large eyes twinkled. "This is going very well," she said.

"So far," Drin said.

"You don't trust them?"

He shook his head. "They're mercenaries. The only saving grace we have is the Sekarans aren't going to pay them more than we are. They're not known for sharing their funds, and they view paid fighters as immoral."

"And you do, too?"

"I do," Drin said. "But my plans and ideas bend to the will of God."

"Do you think we're doing God's will here?"

"I pray so," Drin said, frowning. One of the soldiers approached them then to show them to their guest quarters. Drin motioned for Anais to go ahead of him. She hopped in front of him, chipper as ever. He envied her innocence and her wide-eyed attitude. But he had to stay focused on protecting her.

# FOURTEEN

THE PLANNING SESSION WITH THE MERCENARIES TOOK hours. Anais didn't understand a lot of the specifics, but they covered every detail from how and where to enter the Pyus system, their ship and shuttle trajectories, places where they could avoid detection from the enemy, and more. There was a lot to process, and Anais was glad she had Drin and Jellal to handle all of the information.

After the meeting, the mercenaries showed Anais and Lyssa to sizable quarters meant for dignitaries. The men received their own rooms. She could get used to the larger space to stretch her legs and rest. It hadn't been fun being cooped up in a shuttle or a cell.

Even so, Anais found it difficult to relax. Too many thoughts spun through her mind. What if the Sekarans had blasted Pyus into bits? Or if they had a large force there enslaving her people like the sheiks had done to her when they took her a as a slave on Konsin?

"You alright? You've been sitting staring at your hands for a long time," Lyssa said.

Anais looked up at her friend from where she was seated. "Yeah, just nervous I guess."

"I think we all are. These mercenaries are so thorough, though. I think that's a good thing. Better to be prepared than not."

"When did you get so wise?" Anais smiled.

Lyssa shrugged. "I don't know. Being dragged around and objectified by the Sekarans, it gave me a new perspective on life."

"Me too."

"All we can do is do our best to make a difference, yeah?"

Before Anais could answer, her sensitive ears picked up on a repeating buzzing noise. The guest quarters were positioned to dampen noises like this, but they weren't designed for Pyus ears. "Do you hear that?"

Lyssa cocked her head. "Yeah. Annoying noise."

"Is it some sort of ship alarm, you think?"

"I don't know." Lyssa glanced toward the door. "I'm not sure what we could do about it if it was, though."

Anais pushed herself up out of her seat. "I think I'm gonna go check it out."

"Anais..." Lyssa warned.

"What? If there's something wrong I don't want to end up stuck in these guest quarters. What if we're under attack or if there's an atmosphere leak?" She didn't really like being off-planet. These were things one didn't have to worry about when dirtside.

"Then there's probably not much we can do about it. They'll come for us if we need to evacuate."

"Will they?"

The two women stared at each other. Lyssa shook her head. "I don't know."

"I'll find out. You stay here. You can bet I'll come back for you if there's a problem."

"Be careful."

Anais nodded and made her way for the door. The hallways

had flashing red lights as if to warn the crew. No one was out in the corridors of the guest areas at this time of the night. She'd have to find her way back to where the action was. But where to go?

She found her way to a lift and stepped inside. Instead of calling for one of the specific levels, she waited for someone else to call the car. It moved upward, and the doors opened. Several mercenaries stepped inside.

Anais kept out of their way as they talked, listening to the conversation, trying to be a wallflower and stay unnoticed. If she caused anyone problems, they might report her and confine her to her quarters, and that would defeat the point of her investigating.

"I don't see the point of getting emergency repairs going this late in the night. Why can't it wait until morning?" One of the mercenaries grumbled.

"We didn't sign up for this for an hourly job," one of the others said with a shrug. "Maybe we have to mobilize the fleet quickly."

"Maybe," the first said. He didn't sound convinced or happy about it.

The lift stopped. The doors opened with a *whoosh*. The mercenaries paid her no heed as they exited. Whatever this group was doing, Anais figured they would be in on the action based on what they said. She followed them as they moved down the corridor, ending at a fighter bay. Several dozen other technicians made their way in, while pilots exited.

Everyone moved with urgency. The more Anais watched, the more she saw these people worked hard. All of her worries about mercenaries disappeared. She originally envisioned them to be cutthroats with no honor, especially when they'd thrown them into a cell when they arrived here. Now, it appeared like they functioned with pure discipline. It reminded her of the Elorians. Their movements, their work ethics, were very similar. Even if both groups might not want to be compared to one another.

Dozens of people moved about, all with their own purpose

in what they were doing. It looked like one of their units returned from some mission, but Anais couldn't tell the specifics from her location in the corridor. She didn't dare venture into the fighter bay, because it would likely get her into trouble for being where she didn't belong. What was clear was she and Lyssa wouldn't be in immediate danger. They didn't look like they were in the middle of a battle or prepping to fight, more like trying to recover and make sure their equipment and people were in good shape.

Several medics came out of the fighter bay with stretchers carrying injured mercenaries. There were four of them hurt in all. One of them had burn marks and looked severely wounded. Anais bit her lip after seeing the wound. She'd been exposed to so many injuries recently, but the amount of blood still made her squeamish.

The medics hurried far more than their companions. They had real tasks to perform. Their expressions held fear. The wounds might have been too severe for them to handle.

It dawned on Anais she might be able to help them with their crewmen. She tiptoed around several of the mercenaries, trying not to get in their way, but she also followed the medics. She kept her distance, not sure when the best time to interrupt them would be. When people were in life or death situations, they tended to get snappy.

The medics pushed their stretchers into a lab area. The equipment they had looked less sophisticated than that of the Elorians. They didn't have much fancy machinery. The man who had the worst wounds wailed in pain.

"Someone get him painkillers," one of the medics said.

Another ran to a cabinet, grabbed a hypo, and inserted it into the patient's arm. The injured man's eyes went glassy. He calmed down.

"His wounds are very bad," one of the medics said. "He needs skin grafting, maybe cloned organs. We won't be able to handle it here...maybe if we can get him to the Gykartaway system?"

"I don't think he has that much time."

"A stasis chamber?"

"Do we have a functioning one?"

The medics scrambled trying to see if they had one. They had to attend to their other patients. The mood in the room was dreary, as if no one expected they could actually save the man with the worst wounds.

Anais stepped forward and cleared her throat. "Can I help?"

The medic looked at her like she was crazy. "Who are you?"

"She's one of those visitors Domen's got holed up in the dignitary quarters," another said while he tended to one of the other wounded.

"Thanks, but we're good on personnel here. What we need is better equipment and someone who knows how to manage it," the first said.

"Please, let me try," Anais said.

"What would you suggest we do?" The medic motioned over the man as if to show her it was impossible.

Anais ignored him, breathing slowly. She had to keep her focus to activate the nanites running through her blood. Part of her expected them to stop working at some point, like it was just a dream they were ever there to begin with. She didn't use them very often, especially since they had left.

She stood over the patient. Even though the man now had a hefty dose of painkillers in him, he looked miserable. Death loomed over him like a darkness keeping the room down. But Anais wouldn't let that distract her any more than the medics who naysayed her abilities. She had to keep herself on the task at hand.

The only question she had was this species' anatomy. She didn't recognize what this man was, nor did she know how his internals worked. Would the nanites be able to be effective like they had been with the Elorians? If they had been tailored to Elorian physiology, they might not have been able to meld with her as they did. There was only one way to find out if her abilities could be useful for all species.

All she could do was try.

Anais placed her hands on the injured mercenary's midsection. He squirmed in pain, even through the drugs. The medics around her started shouting at her. "What are you doing?" one of them said. She tuned them out. They didn't matter. They would only be distractions. As she focused, the world around her seemed to disappear. The voices became muffled. The nanites coursed through her—they would flood energy through her hands.

Blinding light poured from her soul through her skin. The people around her would panic even more. They hadn't been used to seeing the energy the Elorian Templars produced. Anais could feel more control this time. It was as if she were directing waves of energy from inside her, changing the flow around her. Would it get easier every time she used these powers?

The nanites engulfed the patient in a shell of light, fluid and yet penetrating. They could sense the injured cells, the tears in his skin and his organs, the burns. They made their repairs. Anais could almost sense every one, down to the smallest molecules. It was different than before, when the healing had stung and taxed her. This feeling was breathtaking. Pure power. God's healing through her. She was one with the universe.

A wide grin crossed her face as the light died out. The time she'd spent in her reverie had been infinite, and she almost lost all sense of herself before returning to this form of reality. When she did, she felt more at peace than ever before. She drew her hands back.

The whole world around her seemed dull. The people, the machinery, the walls, all lifeless colors compared to what she had just experienced. She finally understood why Drin spent so much time in meditation and prayer. When he did battle, did he feel this very thing? He must be constantly striving to recapture it.

She caught herself losing her balance, stumbling backward. One of the other medics braced her by her arm, then looked over to the patient. "His wounds are gone," the medic gasped.

Domen bounded through the doors. He looked like he was about to breathe fire. "Where is he?"

The medics pointed to the man Anais had just healed. Domen brushed past her, moving to his bedside. "His clothes are torn, but he doesn't look bad? I was told this was life-threatening?"

"It was," the first medic said. "This woman healed him. It's a miracle!"

Tears streaked down Domen's face. He wiped them away and sniffled. "I'm sorry. Forgive me. This is my brother. I'd heard he wouldn't make it. Did you really...?"

Anais nodded.

Domen embraced her.

Anais tensed at first, not expecting the hug, but she brought her arms up and returned the gesture. She had no idea who the patient was when she'd initiated the healing. All she wanted was life to keep living.

"Thank you so much. I can't even begin to express what you've done for me," Domen said.

"No problem."

The admiral pulled back from her, meeting out a sigh of relief. "You'd think as a mercenary for so many years, I'd harden myself against pain and death. It never matters when it's family. What happened here?"

The medic told Domen the story. The admiral nodded and listened. "Impressive," Domen said. "Perhaps there's something to Elorian power after all. I'd assumed they simply had military might to be able to impress their myths upon others."

"It's all faith," Anais said. "I didn't believe it at first either."

"Something to think about. Regardless, I'm in your debt. Much more severe debt than a small credit recon assignment. You will have the full might of this fleet if it is needed. You have my word."

Anais wasn't sure what to say. She nodded. This seemed to be a much more personal contract than it had been before. It could only do well for them. "I hope my family can be rescued like your brother," she said, a sudden pang in her heart overwhelming her when she thought of her home. Would they still be alive?

"I hope so as well," Domen said. "Get some rest. We'll all need to be our sharpest when we reach the system tomorrow."

# FIFTEEN

THE MERCENARY BATTLESHIP SLOWED ITS POSITION JUST
outside of the Pyus system, in an area filled with debris. It would
take some intense sensors to take note of them here. Even with
such sensors, they would appear as a distant blip, hardly worth
noting.

Domen had told them the mercs had the sensors to be able to
tell if a large fleet was amassed in orbit of Anais' world. All Drin
and the others could do was wait. They held in their shuttle,
which the mercenaries had outfitted with a sensor-dampening
coating on its hull for when they had to approach the planet.
They'd also given Drin a transponder code to make them appear as
a civilian merchant vessel.

"Domen to shuttle," a voice came through the comm.

Drin tapped the control, glancing at Jellal. "Drin here."

"Our scans of the system show it's fairly clear. If the Sekarans
do have a large force here, they're doing a good job of hiding it,"
Domen said.

"That's good," Anais said from behind Drin. She leaned over

Drin's cockpit chair. Drin would have thought she wanted a better listen, but her ears were better than most. She didn't need to be all that close to him.

The scent of her distracted him. It wasn't as if he found her to be overwhelmingly positive or negative...but he'd become accustomed to her. She had a faint chemical smell about her from her cleaning supplies. It was pleasant. He shook his head to regain his train of thought. "It's good," Drin said, "but it doesn't mean that the surface will be any safer. The Sekarans could very well have left a large force behind and moved onto another system when they found this one to be clear of hostiles."

"Always a downer," Anais said.

"Regardless, you're clear to launch. Our four scouts will help you get a read of the system. Once you're on the ground and you know what the planet's status is, send a signal back to us and we'll do what we can to assist with the rest of the fleet," Domen said.

"Got it," Drin said.

Jellal powered up the shuttle, activating the thrusters to gently lift the ship out of the shuttle bay. Once they were in open space, he pushed the engines a little harder. He waited until they were clear of the larger ship, then activated the hyperdrive.

The hyperspace trip was a quick jump, barely more than a couple of seconds of the flashing light that accompanied such speeds. Jellal dropped them right out again with Pyus encompassing the full view in front of them. The planet was a large one, and they were farther away than it appeared. A small moon blocked the view of a portion of the planet, but most of what they could see was a form of lush greenery. The oceans were a murky blue-gray, but from this distance Pyus looked like a very habitable planet. Much better than the hot, sandy world of Konsin II.

"Recognize anything?" Jellal asked.

Anais pointed forward. "That spot, just above our Mitis moon, it's the Adara continent. That's where I'm from. You can't see it from here because the cities are concealed by the tall forests, but Adara City is right there, too. That's where we'll want to land."

Drin scanned the tactical screen. No large warships, though there were a couple of transports in space near them. Pyus's orbital defenses seemed to be present as well. A dozen satellites with laser beam capabilities. Hopefully, the transponder Domen gave them would provide them enough of a cover to not be targeted by those. Drin flipped the switch to broadcast their ID.

A communication from the planet chirped from the speaker.

"Here we go," Jellal said. He flipped on the comm.

"Transport shuttle *Firebird*, this is Pyus Port Authority. Where's your destination, and what is your business on our world?"

The transponder had worked. Drin leaned back to let Anais do the talking.

"We're heading for Adara City. We're carrying passengers from Parthenon Station," Anais said.

"Very well. You're cleared for landing."

"No wait?" Anais sounded shocked.

"Things have been...a little hectic around here lately. We haven't had nearly as many inbound ships as we used to. You'll see when you arrive. Port Authority out."

The comm signal cut and Jellal was given directions to Adara City's port. The computer took over navigating from there. "That doesn't sound terribly inviting," Jellal said.

"No, it doesn't," Drin agreed.

They approached the world, both of the girls leaning over the piloting chairs. They rocked on their toes, and Drin wished they would sit down. They probably should have with the atmospheric turbulence, but the shuttle's dampeners compensated well as they completed their reentry.

The shuttle descended through the clouds, and over to the lush greenery. It was hard to tell one area from another. There were some open patches, but they were few and far between. As they came closer to the surface, Drin could see how the cities were built out in the trees, buildings weaving through them, sometimes wrapped around the giant greenery. It was odd, spiraling architecture that looked almost like extensions of the trees themselves. It made the forests look all that much thicker.

Until they spotted a smoky area.

Dozens of trees had fallen over, some were incinerated. Buildings had collapsed and were turned into rubble. Several drones and small craft flew around the destruction just up ahead of them. Drin would have asked what happened, but he knew the pattern so well. Sekarans. They torched Adara City while asserting their authority.

Lyssa gasped at the sight. "The trade control center... It's not there."

Anais leaned forward, narrowing her eyes. She turned pale as a ghost. "No, it's not." Tears formed in her eyes. "So many people...I can't believe it."

"Large buildings?" Jellal asked.

"They were a series of five, which stood above all others, representing the five major families of the merchant lords. They shot up above all of the trees. I can't believe they're just...gone."

"It might be dangerous when we get down there," Drin said. "You should cover yourselves. We should too." Drin morphed his nanites into a heavy cloak that came up over his head. Gray, bland, it concealed his green skin and Elorian features. If the Sekarans saw him and Jellal...this wouldn't go well.

Jellal made a similar cloak to Drin's. "Should do well enough."

Anais and Lyssa were out of sorts, hugging each other instead of preparing for landing below. Drin wanted to chastise them, but this was their world, their home. He could only imagine if he returned to the *Justicar* to find it in tatters.

Jellal took the shuttle and found the remains of the spaceport. It was a large open area with a landing pad. He set the ship down. There were several small armored vehicles nearby, as well as a fleet of civilian transports. They must have been the trading vessels the merchant lords used. Drin wanted to ask Anais questions about the world, but she didn't seem like she was in any capacity to give a guided tour. Regardless, she had to get herself together soon.

The shuttle set down on the landing pad. It looked to be about mid-afternoon, but Drin didn't know much about the sun's patterns on this planet. Shadows from the giant trees fell over everything. The landing pad had lights even during the daytime.

The odd part was, the area looked dead. No workers, no one to greet them. They were left alone here, but the port authority had answered them on the comm. Drin opened up the line again. "This is the shuttle *Firebird*. We don't see any docking crews."

"There are no docking crews," the port authority said.

Drin looked back to the two women. "Is this normal?"

Lyssa shook her head. "How do you control the traffic?"

"We don't have much traffic anymore. It's our job to report whether incoming ships look like a threat to the governor. Your small passenger shuttle doesn't pose a threat, so we allowed you to dock. You can leave the area at your leisure," the port authority representative said.

Something didn't feel right to Drin. The Sekarans ran their colonies tightly. "Okay, thank you," he said and cut the comm line.

"You didn't want to find out more?" Anais asked.

Drin stood, causing the women to back up. At the back of the craft sat Err-dio with four mercenaries. "No. We shouldn't alarm them if their job is to report to the Sekarans. It's better to investigate ourselves. Do you have contacts who we should visit?"

"Elaym," Anais said.

Lyssa nodded. "Yes, we should speak with him. He can tell us what happened, and isn't likely to have been targeted since he was just a boy from university, not related to any of the merchant lords. I wish I had my personal comm tablet. All my information would be in there."

"We should go to your former residence first then," Drin said.

Err-dio lowered the back ramp, allowing them all to exit. Each of them grabbed a pack of supplies. It would be better not to leave much with the shuttle in case of looters.

They fanned out into the port area. Everything looked even more dead from the outside than it had from the air. Debris blew across the ground. Several of the largest trees had fallen over some of the roadways. They would have to walk around them.

Anais and Lyssa took lead with Drin and Jellal close behind and the others flanking them. The spaceport's main terminal had most of its windows blown out, glass all over the ground. The insides had been torn apart, looted. He could only have imagined what it once might have looked like, a place of commerce, new. "I hope your whole world's not in this state of devastation," Drin said.

"Me too," Anais said.

The strange, vacant runways of the spaceport dampened the conversation as they walked. Drin kept an eye out in case of attack.

The spaceport was very large, allowing for hundreds of ships to import and export goods at the same time. If the Sekarans had been smart, they would have kept the systems in place. Why hadn't they? This was all too strange.

They passed the entrance where several security vehicles had been left abandoned. The road led into a city amongst the trees, or at least it had been. Several of the trees and buildings looked damaged. Some of the large trees had been uprooted and were falling over, only braced up by other, stronger trees in the forest.

The canopy made for a dark scene, even during the middle of the day. Lights hung from several of the branches, though one in three were out. The entire place appeared to be in disrepair.

"I can't believe this. These streets used to be so busy...so vibrant," Lyssa said.

"Sekaran rule will do that," Jellal said.

Err-dio shook his head. "On Altequine, they enslaved us and worked us hard, but we still had our city squares."

As they ventured into the forest-city, they found some life. Pyus residents might not have been at the spaceport, but they were hard at work in their daily lives. Sekarans stood at busy intersections, armored, laser-repeaters in hand, keeping the peace from their presence. A feeling of darkness loomed everywhere. Even if all of the lights had been on, the sense of foreboding would have remained.

"We have to be careful," Jellal said. "We don't want to draw any Sekaran attention."

"Let's avoid them if possible," Drin said. "They seem to only be in the more heavily populated areas. Are there side streets?"

Anais nodded. "There are. Lyssa, we can take the long way around where the Hidden Oak Club was. Remember?"

"I do," Lyssa said with a faint smile. "I miss those days."

The women led them around a large tree. If the Sekaran guards ahead noticed them, they didn't move from their posts. Sekarans enslaved whole worlds. Everyone appeared to be a slave to them. Only Drin and Jellal's faces would cause concern as Elorians, and they were concealed with their cloaks.

"We used to dance over here," Anais said, pointing to an iron door embedded into a giant trunk. The trunk was bigger than most of the small huts in Altequine. "The club had different floors going up the tree with different themes and music. It was beautiful."

Err-dio glanced up the tree. It stood at least eight stories high and must have been robust if it could be hollowed out and still survive. "The Skree used to have dance circles when tribes would meet. The elders would see how we'd dance, and we'd pick mates. I don't think anyone had any more dancing under Sekaran rule. They frown on such, even though the sheiks had their dancing girls as entertainment. Hypocrites."

Drin didn't say anything. There wasn't much, if any, dancing among the Templars. Some in praise and worship of God, but there were no mating rituals involved.

They continued along. Hovercars and other vehicles buzzed down the streets. Pyus came in different colors than simply white, as Drin saw. Gray, brown, and golden furred people graced the streets.

After another long time of walking, the women complained about getting hungry. Drin directed them into an alleyway between two of the giant trees, minimizing the chance they'd be seen. The trees also provided some nice seating with the roots protruding from the ground. He removed his pack and took out some of the emergency ration bars, distributing one to everyone. In theory, one bar had enough nutrients to sustain a person for a couple of days.

They ate, the women grimacing and complaining about the taste. While they didn't have much flavor, they'd never bothered Drin. Once finished eating—and enjoying a much-needed resting of their feet—the party continued back through the forest-city.

Drin noticed the mercenaries kept amongst themselves, not fraternizing much with Drin and the others. It made sense. They didn't want to grow attached or risk anything going wrong with the job they were hired to do. It made him uneasy, nonetheless. Mercenaries could turn on a person in an instant. It wasn't likely here, especially with Domen's gratitude toward Anais, but it remained possibility nonetheless.

After an hour's walk, they still traveled well in the city's radius, in what looked to be a residential neighborhood. The houses were stacked into the trees, some of them up in the branches themselves with lifts leading upward. Lyssa pointed to one up in the trees. "That's my home. See it?"

She pointed to a single tree with several rooms built into the branches and with a deck built out mid-trunk.

"Lyssa? Is that you?" a voice came from behind them.

Drin spun. The mercenaries stood at the ready. Even though everyone was cloaked and their weapons were well hidden, any one of them could have easily shot down the person talking to them. It was a male Pyus, brown-furred, slightly shorter but stockier than Lyssa or Anais.

"Krytien?" Lyssa rushed forward and gave the man a hug. "I can't believe it."

Drin stood back, watching the interchange as the two reacquainted themselves. Lyssa asked about his family, and Krytien returned with questions of what she had been up to.

"It's a long story," Lyssa said. She turned to Drin and the others. "We just returned to the world. We're trying to figure out what's going on so we can fix things and get them back to normal. I can't believe what we've seen so far."

Krytien's expression flattened. "It's been hard. Things we took for granted are now luxuries. But there's nothing we can do. The Sekarans have all the weapons. They'd overpower us if we tried to resist them."

Anais shook her head. "I know it feels hopeless, but it's not. We've got help." She motioned to Drin and the others. "We need to find Elaym. Do you know where he is?"

Krytien frowned and shook his head. "Perhaps you should come with me. There's a place where the merchant lords' families are hiding. The Sekarans beheaded all of the nobility they could find when they first came here. We did our best to protect the others. If they knew you were here and trying something, it could be very dangerous. Follow me."

The brown Pyus led the way behind a tree. The women trusted him, so Drin and the others followed without protest. He came to a door, which opened into a side room attached to the tree trunk. In the room there was a lift. Once they were all in, the lift didn't go upward, but descended. "Most buildings only go up. The Sekarans won't think to look below ground," Krytien said.

They found their way into an underground passage that led to a shelter, metal construction holding the dirt and tree roots at bay. In contrast to above, it was well-lit and maintained. The shelter had a main room where a dozen Pyus watched the visitors, wide-eyed, frightened.

"Is that Lyssa and Anais?" one of the Pyus asked. The whole group stood and greeted the women with hugs. Anais introduced Drin, Jellal, Err-dio, and the mercenaries, and told the story of how she'd been taken to Altequine, and the subsequent liberation of the planet by the Elorians.

"The Elorians might be our best hope to get out of this alive," Anais said. "But we need to know more of what happened here."

Krytien sighed. "It's a long story. There was a small invasion force the night you were taken. They ransacked your family's palace. Once that force had taken down the primary merchant lord's family, our markets went into chaos. No one could organize. Before we knew it, as second Sekaran invasion force came. This one much bigger. They declared victory within a day, tearing down our buildings as if to show us they could. Some tried to fight, but it was a slaughter.

The Sekarans executed everyone in power they could find. This is all that's left of the merchant lords," Krytien pointed to the others.

"This doesn't look like a standard invasion," Drin said. "Usually, they have a large force. For all of the Sekaran evils, they instill order."

"I don't have much experience with other Sekaran invasions," Krytien said. "But they seemed in a hurry to move on, as if this world meant very little to them. They left a temporary governor. He's not in his right mind. There are rumors he's addicted to nova powder."

Drin had heard of nova powder. Part numbing-agent, part hallucinogenic. None of the Elorians he knew partook in it, but some of the worlds they liberated had an addicted population. It made its users lazy, from what Drin understood. If a Sekaran governor was indeed addicted, it explained a lot. He had a bare amount of order to leech resources from these people but couldn't be bothered to actually run the planet as he should. "I see," Drin said.

"There are also rumors he's only a temporary governor. I don't know how much time we have before a third wave of Sekarans come," Krytien said.

"Elaym," Lyssa said, interrupting the conversation. "Did he make it?"

"He did," Krytien said. "Except he's been kidnapped—he's beingheld in the old psychiatric ward. The Sekarans converted it into a prison. He knows about some of our hideaways, but not this one. We moved everyone as soon as the word came down. They'll be using him for information and will probably kill him once they find he has none that's useful."

"This is all so much to process," Anais said.

"Indeed," Drin said. "We're weary from travel. Let's sit, talk, and rest. Anything you can tell us about how many Sekarans are here on the planet, where they're stationed, and what their standard movements are like will help us to determine our next course of action."

The Pyus merchant lords in the room muttered to themselves.

They acted in disbelief. Drin knew they wondered how such a small force could do anything. Their faith in life had been broken by the Sekarans. Drin and Jellal would have their work cut out for them to restore it and, hopefully, bring a new faith to them in the process. One much more solid than the consumerism these people once worshiped.

# SIXTEEN

"THESE PEOPLE NEED FAITH IF THEY EVER EXPECT THE LORD to grant them a victory," Jellal said, pacing the small room he shared with Drin.

Anais stood by the wall, listening to the two Elorians discuss their plans. The mercenaries were given their own space apart from them, leaving them to be able to talk alone.

Anais and Lyssa were supposed to stay with the other merchant lords, in theory. While Lyssa likely would remain in the underground compound, Anais itched to mount a rescue effort of Elaym. They couldn't leave him in the clutches of these evil Sekarans. If they tortured him for information, his suffering would be indescribable. Anais knew firsthand how they treated their slaves in an inhumane manner.

Drin shook his head, sitting on the bottom bunk of a double cot. He had his hands folded in his lap. "Now isn't the time, Jellal. Their hearts need to be open. I went through this with the Skree. When they are receptive to the message, that is when you'll change hearts."

"I was there when Drin spoke," Err-dio said. "It was because we asked him. He didn't force his messages on us."

"But nothing can be accomplished without faith. How are we supposed to wage a holy war without the faithful?" Jellal slapped his hand on his leg, frustrated.

"*We* are the faithful," Drin said. "By our deeds they'll know us."

Anais had been watching them go on like this for a while. Jellal had less patience than Drin from what she'd seen. She was glad it hadn't been him who'd rescued her from the Sekarans originally. She might not have been as receptive to the tales of the Elorian God if Jellal had.

Nanites coursed through her veins, reminding her of the very real, tangible gifts Drin bestowed upon her. But those were an anomaly. Most non-Elorians never received the technological wonders that reshaped battles. They could only gain faith by seeing it on display in others.

"If we rescue Elaym, it will ingratiate you to the merchant lords here," Anais said, hoping to sound half as persuasive as Lyssa did when she negotiated with others.

Drin and Jellal were the best hope to save Elaym. Before it was too late.

"I'm not sure that's the wisest course, either," Drin said, frowning. "If we mount a rescue mission, it will alert the Sekarans to the presence of Templars."

"Only if we're not careful," Jellal said. "I think the woman's right. Give the people here something to believe in. It's the way we can foster the message and save their souls."

Silence fell between the two men. Jellal's gaze was almost challenging. Anais wondered if she would have to break the two up. Elorians were such intense people in their faith and their constant battling.

"Elaym will be important to the morale of everyone here, Drin," she nudged again.

"What do we know of this psychiatric ward?" Drin asked. "How fortified is it? We still haven't gotten much of a lay of the land. The Pyus make it sound like there isn't much of a Sekaran force, but I don't want to underestimate them as they do us."

"Going out and seeing for ourselves will be the only way to ascertain their real strengths and positioning. We can send the mercenaries throughout the city to make detailed notes on Sekaran whereabouts before we go," Jellal said.

"At the very least, we'll have to do that," Drin agreed.

"Then we're going to rescue Elaym?" Anais asked, hopeful.

"I'm considering it," Drin said. "Let's do as Jellal said and find the positions of the Sekarans before deciding."

Err-dio stood. "I'll summon the mercenaries."

He left the room and returned with the four Sagitars. Drin explained to them what was needed, and the merchant lords provided the mercenaries with maps of the city. It sounded like a simple mission. If they split up, they could easily act as traders if the Sekarans decided to question them.

The mercenaries were prepared for the mission and dispersed after receiving their instructions. Drin and Jellal didn't dare go out and perform the recon mission themselves, as they would be easily spotted as Elorians. If the Sekarans realized their sworn enemies were on the planet, it would change the whole dynamic of the situation, and not for the better. They would be on alert.

Anais decided to pass the time by reading more of Marayh.

The famous Elorian woman came into following Yezuah when he first appeared to the twelve tribes. She was a prostitute among the Durbian tribe, providing comfort to the soldiers during the endless battles of the Hundred Years War. Their tribe had been hit the hardest, with fertile lands making for a prime target for the other neighboring tribes to hit, especially during harvest seasons. Everyone was short on food and supplies, and in this season, a plague of locusts had descended upon the farmlands, making food even more scarce.

When Marayh saw Yezuah, she fell at his feet. So many were falling sick from the food they were eating, the locusts spreading disease across everything. Yezuah took pity on her, telling her to rise and sin no more. She would be the mother among the soldiers, providing comfort in new ways.

At first, Marayh didn't notice much of any change, but she knew Yezuah to be the Lord by his presence, the man who would fulfill prophecy. Her faith was strong.

She came across a wounded soldier on the road, left to die as he wasn't able to walk. She took pity on him, offering water. That's when she found her powers starting to manifest from the nanites that had been, unbeknownst to her, bestowed upon her. She touched the soldier, and glowing light came from her hands. The man who would surely have died before had been shown compassion, and he was healed. He rose to his feet and promised to deliver word of Yezuah to his tribe.

Word of her miracles spread, and soon, many people came to Marayh for healing. Yezuah had moved on to other tribes at the time to show them his wonders, but Marayh became his first disciple, often forgotten in that fact because so many generals and soldiers soon came to follow Yezuah. She went on to heal the plague facing the Durbian tribe, cleansing the food, and making it safe to eat. No one became sick any longer.

Anais blinked as she turned the page and finished a chapter. "What am I supposed to glean from this?"

"What are you reading?" Drin asked.

"The Gospel of Marayh," Anais said.

"Apocrypha," Jellal said.

Drin took in a deep breath. "Just because a writing hasn't been canonized doesn't mean it's worthless. What did you learn about her?"

Anais told him of the miracles and healings Marayh had performed.

Drin nodded. "It sounds like her immense faith changed the course of an entire tribe."

Anais considered his words. Could she have that kind of faith? She didn't seem to feel it like Drin and Jellal did. She had to believe in Yezuah. All she had seen had been miraculous enough, but she didn't have the kind of *passion* they did. Could she ever attain it? Did she need to?

"Something to pray and reflect on," Drin said. He lifted his head toward the opening in the room. The mercenaries had returned.

One of the mercenaries approached Drin and saluted him. The others produced their datapads with maps, coordinates. They were extremely detailed with positions of Sekaran guard units, even listing some of their patrols from what they'd found. The mercenaries impressed Anais. She couldn't have imagined accumulating all of that information so quickly. Jellal and Err-dio watched as the mercenaries laid out the entire city.

Anais pointed to the asylum. "Look. It's not that heavily guarded," she said. Hope filled her for the first time since she'd arrived on her world. If they could rescue Elaym, they might have a shot at restoring Pyus to some sanity. "We can do this."

Drin studied the map carefully but didn't respond. It was as if he were lost in his own world. His brows furrowed in an intense way Anais had become fond of. His seriousness probably wouldn't be popular among most of the Pyus, but she found it endearing. He cared.

After a while, he nodded to himself. "We can attempt a rescue. I think it would be best to try to minimize our exposure. Jellal and I will do this on our own."

"Agreed," Jellal said.

Err-dio frowned. "But, Templar, sir, as your squire, I—"

Drin held up a hand to cut him off. "You don't have the nanites running through your blood that I do. Which means you wouldn't have the shielding capabilities I do. Your presence would be a liability, and with more foreigners walking around, the odds of exposure increases as well."

Judging by the expression on his face, Err-dio didn't seem to like the comment. He pressed his lips together and nodded, nonetheless.

"You could use a local guide, though. It might be helpful to have someone along in case you do get spotted as foreigners," Anais said.

Drin narrowed his eyes at her. "I don't think it's wise for you to be near an impending battle."

"I have nanite protection just like you do," Anais said, crossing her arms over her chest.

Drin sighed. "So you do. Very well, you can come with us, but I want you to be careful. No rushing out into the enemy...or doing anything else that would be, ah—"

"Stupid?" Anais asked.

"I was trying to find a more diplomatic word."

"No need to mince words with me. I've had quite enough of lessons because of the stupid things I've done. You can count on me," Anais said.

"Very well." Drin stood. He pointed to the mercenaries and Err-dio. "Your mission is to make sure everyone here remains safe. These aren't people experienced with combat, or with being in hiding for that matter. Advise them, but be patient. We have a long road ahead of us, and if we have any chance at liberating this world, we're going to need the support of the people hiding underground here. Understood?"

"Yes, sir," the mercenaries and Err-dio said in unison.

Jellal stretched his arms above his head. "When do we leave?"

"We wait until nightfall. That way we'll be concealed as best as can be. Until then, we pray." Drin left the room, followed by Jellal. They would probably find somewhere solitary to meditate and pray.

Anais considered joining them, but she wanted to talk to some of the other merchant lords. It had been so long. Her prayers couldn't matter that much, could they? Guilt tugged at her heart, but she couldn't say why. She shook her head and did her best to ignore the feeling before heading to the main room to talk with the others.

# SEVENTEEN

DRIN APPROACHED THE ASYLUM COMPOUND WITH ANAIS AT the lead and Jellal beside him. Drin watched the girl carefully. Even though she was no longer a prisoner on a strange world, he couldn't help but feel a strange obligation to protect her. She didn't likely need it on this world, in this city, where she knew her way around. The streets were familiar to her. It was Drin and Jellal who were the foreigners here.

The asylum was gated. Dark metal poles comprised a fence around the large ward, a building constructed between four of the giant trees, and having extensions up into their branches. The gates were shut for the evening, one of the hazards of their plan. Drin, Jellal, and Anais stopped at another large tree, several meters away, in order to take cover and assess the situation. No guards seemed to be present near the front of the compound, though lights were on inside. Other lights flickered along a dim path to the front of the building. They would have to avoid the path if possible.

"We leap over fence?" Jellal asked, his voice just above a whisper.

"Seems to be the only way inside. Once in, we should look for a side or maintenance entrance if we can find one."

Anais' ear twitched. "How are we supposed to leap over that? It's tall, and there's no way to get a foothold to get up."

"The nanites," Drin said. "We use them to boost ourselves over."

"I don't know how to do that," Anais said.

Drin chided himself for allowing the girl to come with them. She didn't have any combat experience, and listening to her pleas had been a lapse in judgment. He had a hard time saying no to her, however. It was his own failing. Something he would beg the Lord forgiveness for later. "You concentrate just like when forming a sword or armor. At the moment you're about to jump, you do it."

"I'll go first and show you," Jellal said.

Jellal stepped out from behind the cover, getting into a position to run, and then he took off. He moved with elegant speed, nanites assisting him even in his basic steps. Once he came close to the fence, he leapt, and in doing so, cleared the fence by at least twice over. His landing was clean, on both feet, and he turned around to look at them before concealing himself in the darkness of the asylum's compound.

"You understand?" Drin asked.

"I think so."

"Good," Drin said. Without further word, he took off running after Jellal. The wind kissed his face. He loved getting the speed the nanites provided. It made him feel alive. The tiny bots coursing through his veins seemed to invigorate every aspect of his being. When he came close, he bent his knees and jumped, his ascent taking him higher than Jellal's had. It wasn't a competition, but Drin liked to show his brother exactly the extent of his skills. He ended up so high that he was able to get a grip on one of the tree branches. Once steady, he let himself drop into an easy fall, turning to see Anais.

She hadn't moved yet, still hiding behind her cover. Drin motioned to her to try to get her to make her way forward, but he couldn't call to her. It might alert someone inside.

After several moments of hesitation, Anais tepidly moved forward. She wasn't gaining enough speed. The woman didn't have the confidence with the nanites he and Jellal had. She approached the gate nonetheless, keeping her head down. The nanites weren't assisting her movement. Only her natural speed brought her toward the gate, faster than any other sentient beings Drin had seen, but still not fast enough. She jumped...

...and collided with the gate. Several curses escaped her lips as she backed away from the gate.

"Hurry. And don't make so much noise," Jellal whispered.

She took a deep breath and stepped back once more. This time, she didn't have nearly as much of a lead up to the fence as before, but the nanites activated. Subtle pink bolts of electricity trickled down her legs to her feet. She glowed with energy as she took off from the ground. She didn't make it nearly as high as Drin or even Jellal had, but she cleared the fence, hitting dirt on the other side and landing in a run. Her momentum carried her forward toward Drin, who caught her in his arms.

"Careful," Drin said, steadying her.

"I did it." Anais looked up at him, wide-eyed.

Drin turned away before he became tempted to stare into those eyes for too long. "Good work. Now let's see if we can find another entrance."

The three of them circled around the asylum, careful in their steps not to make too much noise. No one was outside, but they didn't need to alert anyone either. Jellal stopped in front of a window, slightly higher than they could reach. It was cracked open. "This would be a good way inside." Jellal turned to Drin and Anais. "Do you think she can jump and pull herself up?"

Drin frowned, looking up at the aperture. Anais wasn't reliable enough with the use of her nanites yet to guarantee she'd make it. Making a quick decision, he crouched down. "Get up on my shoulders," he said while motioning to Jellal to move up.

Jellal made the jump up to the window and crawled inside.

"You're not going to jump up there with me?" Anais asked. She moved toward him and wrapped her legs around his shoulders.

Drin tried his best to ignore her form, to ignore the touch. It was all too much. This was exactly what he wanted to avoid. He should have had Jellal perform this task.

It was too late to second guess. He felt her warm body on him but stood, nonetheless. She gripped onto his cloak to keep a balance.

"Now stand," Drin said.

"Oh," Anais said. She wobbled atop him, getting to her knees first, barely able to maintain her balance. Drin had to keep her in place with his hands, which didn't help the lustful thoughts already seeping into his consciousness. *Why, Yezuah, would you test me like this?*

It seemed like an eternity before she made it to her feet. "Get her, Jellal," Drin said.

Soon, the weight of her was off his shoulders. Drin looked up to see Anais being pulled through the window. He took a deep breath to clear his head. Search and rescue. Focus. He crouched down, and with the power of the nanites, leapt upward again. Gripping the window sill, he pulled himself inside.

The asylum was dimly lit. The three of them found themselves in a hallway with wooden floors, no decorations on the walls. They'd be on the second level. But how many levels were there to the building? They had to search and find this Elaym quickly. Drin looked to Anais. "Now what?"

"I haven't been here before," she said, whispering. "This is where they keep the extremely ill patients." She spun, reading the signs on the walls, and made slow steps forward.

The three of them moved forward, Drin and Jellal carefully guarding Anais. She had nanites of her own, but she couldn't be trusted to use them.

The hallway was tight, eerily empty in the evening. Shadows fell through the windows from the trees outside. They came to a room that had no windows. Drin tried the door. It was sealed shut.

"Back up," Drin said, forming his light sword into his hand. He carefully cut through the door, piercing the area where the dead-bolt must have been. The door popped open.

Inside sat a single Pyus. A male, judging from his stockier build. The Pyus male scrambled to his feet. "Who..."

"We're here to rescue you," Anais said, pushing past Drin and Jellal. "Though I'm not sure who you are. What happened here?"

"My name is Antin," the man said. "I ran security for the Woodburn family."

"I'm Carver," Anais said.

Antin nodded. "It's good to see some of the merchant lords survived. Who are your friends?"

Anais glanced back at Drin and Jellal. "They're here to help. Do you know what's going on? Elaym was supposed to be held at this facility."

"I'd heard they took him into deep interrogation. The Sekaran governor here is drugged out of his mind. That's why everything's in such disarray. Most of us here they leave to—"

Laser-repeater bolts came blasting into the room from behind them. One hit Antin between the eyes. He crumpled to the floor.

Drin spun, grateful the light sword was already active in his hand. Sekaran guards in full battle armor stood in the hallway. They had their laser-repeaters jammed into the doorway. They fired several bolts, the energy dissipating into the nanite shields Drin and Jellal had.

Jellal pushed forward, blocking the doorway from any fire reaching inside. He activated his light sword, slicing through three

Sekarans, but more came. They'd been caught. Someone had mobilized a full guard force against them. As soon as Jellal cut one down, two more appeared. It would be hard to get out of here.

Drin glanced around the room. There was no other way out. The walls were padded. He moved to the back wall, pushing his light sword through it. He could cut a secondary exit, give a way for the three of them to escape that wouldn't be blocked by Sekarans.

"What can I do to help?" Anais said, stepping to Drin's side.

"Keep out of the way," Drin said. He grimaced. The wall was made of some thick metal, which made it difficult to cut through, even with the guidance of the nanites. The sword felt real in his hand, and the drag against the energy was the same as if he had a physical blade.

He'd managed to cut one line before Jellal fell back into the room. The Sekarans pushed them backward, using shields of their own that his light sword couldn't penetrate. They didn't dare get too close like their fallen compatriots. They were learning.

"How's your shield energy," Drin asked.

"Holding," Jellal said. "Just hurry."

Drin didn't bother looking back at Jellal and assumed his brother didn't give him a glance either. They knew each other well enough to predict each other's actions in battle. His blade cut through the next line of the wall. Two done, two to go until he could punch a hole in it and escape. He drew his blade upward for the third cut.

"Give up!" shouted a booming voice from the hallway. "You have no escape and you're outnumbered."

"Numbers don't matter when the Lord is with us!" Jellal shouted back.

Something hit the ground in the room, causing Drin to look back. It was a small grenade. He'd seen its type before, and his eyes went wide. "EMP," Drin said to warn his friends.

The grenade went off in a blinding flash. Jellal's nanites all collapsed, the pink energy dissipating, and the nanites outside of his body falling to the ground like dust. His blade shimmered out of existence.

Drin's weapon also disappeared, though he had nearly completed the fourth cut in the wall. He kicked the wall in the rest of the way, and it gave, creating an exit to the outside.

He turned to assist his friend, but it was too late. Laser-repeater bolts pummeled into Jellal. He collapsed to his knees, blood pouring from him. "Lord...forgive me..." he choked out before falling face forward.

"Jellal!" Drin shouted. He clenched his teeth to fight back tears. He couldn't spend time thinking about his fallen friend. Not now.

Anais screamed. Sekaran guards flooded into the room. As she was no threat, they grabbed her.

Drin had a decision to make. His nanites were dead, at least for now, until he could find a way to recharge them. "Anais," he said.

"Go!" she shouted back at him, flailing her arms at the guards and forcing them to fall over. They hadn't expected such resistance from her. She didn't stop there either. Anais jumped on the guards so they couldn't regain their footing, giving Drin ample room to escape.

He hated leaving the battle. It flew against every fiber of his being to leave her there, but he could do no good for her. She made a valiant effort defending him so he could escape. He couldn't waste it.

Instead of spending more time deliberating, Drin ducked through the hole in the wall, crouching, and jumping down a story to the grass outside. He fell into a roll when he landed and took off toward the fence. Without nanites, he would have to try to climb it the old-fashioned way. He jumped as high as he could, relying on his strength to get him to a point where he could get a grip up top.

He succeeded, clutching the top of the fence. Laser-bolts blasted from the building behind him, but they missed. He leaped over the wall and ran away from the scene. He cursed himself for not planning the assault better. They'd rushed into action in their overconfidence, thinking their technology could overcome any Sekaran resistance. They should have known better. The Lord gave warnings about such arrogance when he'd spoken to the twelve tribes of Eloria.

But it didn't matter now. Jellal was gone. Lord, how could that have happened? They'd been faithful during this entire expedition. They hadn't forgotten prayers. Jellal perhaps more than Drin had displayed immense faith. It wasn't fair. Drin wished the Lord took him instead of his brother.

Worse, the Sekarans had Anais. She'd been valiant in what she'd done. Did she have the wherewithal to understand the battle, how his survival meant so much to the overall effort? He had to regroup with her friends and the mercenaries and figure out how to rescue her. He could only pray the Sekarans wouldn't be too cruel to her. Drin muttered those prayers to himself as he ran through the Pyus forest-city.

# EIGHTEEN

THE SEKARAN SOLDIERS DRAGGED ANAIS DOWN THE hallway. They had her by each arm, letting her feet dangle as she faced backwards. The nanites inside her had all but dissipated. She couldn't feel them anymore. What had they set off in there? Was this what Drin had felt before when he'd returned from his mission on Konsin with dead nanites?

Anais took a deep breath as they took her away. She closed her eyes, focusing. There had to be something there. She tried to will the nanites to surround her.

Nothing happened.

The soldiers took her down the stairs, her feet clanking on each step as they descended. She finally opened her eyes again. This didn't bode well. If Drin made it out, maybe he could get help from the mercenaries. She had to hope he made it.

Her mind flashed the image of Jellal on the floor of the psychiatric cell, full of holes from the laser-repeater bolts. Part of her couldn't believe it had happened. She'd seen Drin downed in battle before when a battlemage nearly overpowered him, but it often felt like the Templars were invincible. At least, they should have been. But they could die just as easily as anyone else without the power of their nanites.

It left her with one Templar and a handful of mercenaries to liberate her world. They'd been too overconfident in thinking they could descend on Pyus alone and make headway against the Sekarans.

The soldiers took her out of the psychiatric ward. They opened the gate and dragged her through the streets. Other Pyus kept their heads down, even as they tried to look out of the corner of their eyes to see what transpired. No one wanted to risk getting the same treatment she did. It infuriated her. Why wouldn't they fight, try to do something?

But then, she couldn't expect a bunch of civilians—people who had been just like she was less than a year ago—to have a natural desire to fight against a force like the Sekarans. It would be too risky for anyone to try to do anything. They'd get shot down just like Jellal.

It was hopeless. Her heart sank. All of the work they'd put in so far, all of the pushing to get here, and she had no real way to help her people.

Tears formed in her eyes, but she refused to cry. She couldn't wipe them away with the soldiers holding her arms back. The moisture in her eyes irritated her, stinging in the night air.

They crossed a few streets and came to a large residence. Anais turned her head back around to get a good look, and her eyes went wide as the gates opened. This was her former home. The House of Carver, where her family lived and conducted their trade as the most powerful merchant family on Pyus. It was a large house, with round wings wrapping around multiple trees. Her family had painted it white but now it was sullied by the recent occupation with dirt and debris on its walls. Lights shone on it in the evening, a beacon within the forest, a symbol of Pyus prosperity. At least, it had been.

Several more soldiers stood guard at the residence. Despite so many people out at this time of the evening, it felt like the place was empty. The fountains didn't run. The gardens were overgrown, full of weeds, and several of the unattended plantings were dead. There'd been little attention spent on the maintenance of the place. Her home was the ghost of its former self.

Anais remembered running up the front steps where the soldiers now dragged her. She'd run in on her way back from school, her chef always ready with a tasty snack. Not this time.

Her stomach grumbled, reminding her she hadn't eaten anything in hours, and even then, it had been those near-tasteless Elorian rations.

The soldiers dragged her through the arched front door. The main entrance looked much as she'd remembered it, a large mirror hanging by the back stairwell, several paintings of her family's history on the wall, a large vase, but instead of the purple rain flower that was there before, no plant was in it. It must have died from lack of care along with so many of the plants in the garden.

They turned into the main reception room. A fireplace at the back burned with a warm fire that heated the room. Several chairs lined the room, from wooden decorative chairs to leather ones for comfort while sitting in front of the fire. An ornate rug lined the floor, complete with pictures woven into the fabric detailing the first trade deals between Pyus and off-worlders hundreds of years ago. Seeing it brought Anais a feeling of comfort she hadn't had in a long time. This was her home...but her family wasn't here.

A muscular Sekaran man in a long red robe stood, facing the fire. Black hair curled down to the small of his back. He turned. He had a pipe in his mouth and blew smoke out of it. Red, beady eyes honed in on Anais. He glanced at her like an object, nothing more, and the way he looked at her shook her.

Her jaw dropped.

"Strip her," the man said. The guards moved from her sides

and tore at her clothes. Anais didn't bother to resist. She'd been in this position before. Fighting would only get the Sekarans more excited, something she didn't want. She had no shame any longer. It wasn't the first time Sekarans had torn her clothes away from her. She didn't bother to cover herself or recoil. Perhaps it was her being too used to this kind of treatment by Sekarans, an ugly thing, but she just cast her eyes low and stood still.

The robed man walked up to her, inspecting her like several Sekaran lords had done before. She'd been named a slave, forced to be a dancing girl for a Sekaran battlemage. What would this Sekaran demand of her?

He held her chin up, forcing her to look into his eyes. Anais didn't quiver. These people only respected strength. She'd seen that enough in them.

The man's eyes were glassy now that she looked at them, as if he weren't all there. He grinned as if he found something extremely funny. "This one has been through a lot," the robed Sekaran said. "What is your name?"

"Anais," she said.

"I am Jafil, governor of this world. *Your* world." He spun away from her, puffing on his pipe again. "You're to be my second slave. I don't know what you've done, or why. Frankly, I don't care. I need good help around here...and Pyus women are delightful to look at. Especially in your natural fur."

Anais said nothing. He didn't seem overly aggressive. That was good, at least.

Jafil stumbled. Several of the guards in the room moved over to help him, but he righted himself before they could reach him. "I'm fine, I'm fine. The dust makes me forget about gravity sometimes." He smacked his lips.

Then, in a sudden turn of mood, he frowned deeply, letting himself fall into one of the leather chairs.

"Shall I take her away then and get her situated in the servants' wing?" One of the guards asked.

"No, leave her here. You leave, though. Seeing warriors is reminding me of so much bloodshed."

A Sekaran worried about bloodshed? Anais couldn't hide the confusion on her face as she looked over at the guard Jafil spoke with.

The guard seemed to be just as confused as she was by his expression. But he shook his head. "As you wish, Governor," the guard said. He stepped backward, motioning to the others, and they departed the room, leaving Anais with this strange governor.

She wasn't sure what she was supposed to do. The room fell quiet except for the flicker of the fire in the opposite corner, where the governor sat staring. The flames cast an ominous shadow on his face, where he blew yet more smoke out of the pipe.

"Might I confess something to you?" he said finally, breaking the silence.

"Uh...sure," Anais said, taking a light step forward. It was strange having him not face her when he spoke. He'd had her stripped naked just to look away? Nothing about this encounter made sense. She recalled he'd mentioned dust. What did he mean by that?

"This assignment was supposed to be temporary. I was to hold this world while my people reassessed their strategies. And they left me here. There's no word of return, and my son has contracted some rare disease from these parts. I'm helpless to do anything. It's just party after party, night after night... bwah!" Jafil burst into crazed laughter.

Anais backpedaled, erasing her prior steps forward. This was a madman, and he was in charge of her whole world. No wonder the city seemed so disheveled, why trade had all but ceased, and business was conducted so haphazardly. The damage this temporary governor had done could take years to repair. But she had to reclaim Pyus first. Right now, she wasn't in much of a position to do much of anything, standing naked and enslaved before this man.

Should she try to kill him? It caused her to shiver, thinking that thought, and she covered her breasts with her arms. How could she think such violent thoughts? But she'd been here before, been so mad. This captor wouldn't be much of a match for her, with the guards outside, and him seeming to be intoxicated.

"You're thinking about harming me," Jafil said, sliding around in the chair to face her, draping one leg over the arm of the chair. "I can sense it. I can *feel* it. His eyes looked much larger than they had the first time he'd looked at her.

"I—"

"No sense in lying. I can tell. The dust. It makes me see things."

*Great*, thought Anais.

"The guards are just outside. You wouldn't get very far. And if you'd managed to harm me, someone far worse would likely take my place. He wouldn't be so kind to your people. All I've done is round up any of the leaders and the insurgents." He smacked his lips again. "I've been downright kind."

"You...mentioned a son?" Anais said, trying to divert the conversation.

Jafil frowned. "Yes. He won't be for this life much longer. This accursed world."

"Perhaps I can help?" Anais said. She still couldn't feel the nanites in her. Whatever had gone off in the psychiatric ward had lasting effects, it seemed. When Drin had lost his nanites the last time, it took hers interacting with him to activate them. She didn't have that option anymore, did she? The only Elorians on the planet were dead...or in the same situation as she was. *If* Drin had escaped. She glanced back over her shoulder instinctively, wishing he were there with her.

"You?" Jafil laughed. "I very much doubt you'd be in a position to do much. Where did you come from, anyway? My men only informed me they'd captured someone trying to break into one of our facilities."

"I was in the psychiatric ward," Anais said.

"Ah," Jafil said. "Why? Are you a mental patient?"

"I broke in,"

Silence fell again. Jafil looked as if he were making a very important decision. "I am very desperate to help my son. You may not be on dust, but you sensed that right. And I sense you're being forthright with me."

"You told me not to bother lying." Anais shrugged.

"So I did. And you listened. I like that!" He cackled again.

"Do you want me to help him?" Anais asked.

Jafil brought his hand to his chin and stroked it. "Depends, what would you want in exchange?"

"I'd want to be released, and I'd like you to also release your prisoner, Elaym."

"Elaym...Elaym..." Jafil's brow furrowed as he said the name, his glassy eyes scanning as if he were trying to recall where he had heard the name. He snapped his fingers. "Ah! The merchant lord boy. He's been delightful to interrogate, so my people tell me. Gives up information without much of a fuss at all. Wouldn't it be nice if all subjects were like that?" Jafil stood, pacing toward Anais. She tensed as he came closer, but he laughed at it, flicking her in the nose. "You're so jumpy, even though you pretend to be strong. It would be very fun having you around here, I see. Very fun. Alas, I'll consider your request."

Anais let out a breath she hadn't realized she'd been holding. He wasn't going to hurt her, at least not yet. Whatever substance this dust was made his moods swing rapidly. She couldn't trust anything he said. "Thank you."

Jafil raised his head and shouted. "Guards! Retrieve the new slave!"

The guards poured back into the room. They grabbed her with as much forcefulness as they had when they first had captured her and carried her away.

# NINETEEN

DRIN SAT WITH HIS EYES CLOSED, LEGS IN A CROSSED position, hands on his knees. It was the position of prayer, focus, and meditation. Yet try as he might, he couldn't keep his mind on the Lord. His thoughts kept reverting to watching his brother Jellal getting pierced by laser-repeater bolts, falling, collapsing, dying. Why hadn't God saved him? Why did He allow for this to happen to one of his faithful? It wasn't fair. It wasn't right. Drin dug his fingertips into his leg, frustrated. He wanted to lash out, to break things, to do violence.

Rage wasn't healthy. It wasn't of the Lord. He understood God meant love. Intellectually, he knew bad things happened because of the evil in this fallen universe, dating back to the beginning of creation, when Elorians tried to taste the fruit of knowledge. When they'd become sinners in the first place.

*Forgive me, Lord, for my unfaithfulness.*

The prayer calmed Drin. At least to some extent. He couldn't change the events that had occurred, only the future. And he would change the future, even if he didn't know specifically what to do at this time. He prayed for guidance. A sign. Anything.

The door to the room creaked. Drin opened his eyes.

Err-dio stood in the doorway. "I apologize, Templar. Did I interrupt your prayers?"

"You did," Drin said. His words came out all too cold. Err-dio wanted to serve him, to help the cause, to do the Lord's work. He should be kinder to the Skree.

"My apologies, Templar." Err-dio bowed his head low.

"Think nothing of it. What do you need, my friend?"

Err-dio lifted his head once more. "I just wanted to see what you thought our next move was."

"To be honest, I don't know."

The Skree's expression went flat. Drin could tell he was disappointed, but what else could he do? "I see," Err-dio said.

"The Sekaran presence here is stronger than we anticipated based on the mercenaries' original assessment," Drin said.

"We have to get Anais back," Err-dio said. "She was there for us."

"She was. And we do."

"Do we need to pray more?"

"It's always a good idea," Drin said.

Err-dio looked confused, glancing behind him. "Well...I'll do my best. I'll leave you to your prayers, then."

"Wait," Drin said, holding a hand up. "I've been praying this entire time. We need a much more superior force than we have. If we could somehow summon the mercenary fleet and convince them to come, perhaps we can end this quickly."

"Let's talk to Krytien and see if he can let us send a signal." Err-dio moved to Drin and offered him a hand up.

Drin took his hand and stood with a grunt. Everything required so much more effort without the nanites. What he needed to do was pray, focus on the machines, and hope that the Lord would restore them. It was another problem he had no means to solve.

They entered the main room where the Pyus merchant lords had gathered. Most of the Pyus watched various feeds of their planet, monitoring, taking notes, gathering information in hopes that what they did would have a positive impact. Krytien looked to Drin as soon as he arrived. His eyes were hopeful. "Elorian," Krytien said.

"Hello," Drin said.

"Did you have a good...prayer session? Is that what you call it?"

"Right enough," Drin said. "I cleared my head some. It was hard losing someone I considered a brother."

Krytien cast his eyes downward. "I know. I lost my own to the Sekarans when they invaded."

"My condolences," Drin said.

The Pyus man nodded to him in understanding. "What can I help you with then?"

Err-dio stepped forward. "We need to open a line of communications to our mercenary fleet and hail Admiral Domen."

Drin nodded.

"I'm afraid that's going to be impossible," Krytien said.

"Why's that?" Drin asked.

"When you and Anais had your encounter with the Sekarans, they raised a signal-scattering field around the planet. There's no way to get communications in or out."

"Which means they can't contact their fleet either," Err-dio said.

Drin stared at the screen in front of him, which displayed the city's streets. It was early morning. The Pyus population scurried about, heading to their daily lives. While the war had impacted some people, it didn't all. Or did it? Drin could hardly tell what was forced labor or not from a small feed. "I suppose that's one small blessing. Thank you, Err-dio, for reminding us. But still, if we're going to save this planet, we're going to need to contact our own reinforcements."

"Should we try to find the source of their scattering field and knock it out?" Krytien asked.

It was a good idea, but if they didn't have the manpower to even break a single person out of a psychiatric ward, could they hope to bring down one of the Sekarans' actual defense points? It would likely prove to be more heavily guarded.

Drin shook his head. "No. Our best option will be to go up in our shuttle and try to get past the field and contact our allies." *And hope that they aren't afraid of engaging the Sekarans on the ground.* One could never tell with mercenaries how reliable they would be, even if Admiral Domen seemed to have sympathy toward Anais and her cause.

"Will that be safe?"

"They allowed us to set down without hassling us," Drin said. "We'll have to hope they'll cause no problems for us when we take off."

Drin's eyes went wide, and he stifled a breath. He felt something stirring within him. It was like a rush of blood to the head. But he knew it was far more than that. The nanites. They were reactivating. Whatever had hit him hadn't done permanent damage.

"Elorian? Is everything okay?" Krytien asked.

Drin stumbled backward. It was difficult to keep his balance as the nanites returned to life within him. One after another, they came to life. He could sense them and their net growing. Like waking up, at first the control was sluggish, but then it returned. It had to be a sign, one that they were on the right track. "Everything is better than okay. Praise Yezuah. I'm going to return to my prayers, and we will make for the spaceport when I am done."

The Pyus looked on with skepticism. How could he blame them? He must have looked crazy from their perspectives. But his power was returning. Perhaps this fight wouldn't be hopeless after all.

# TWENTY

A SEKARAN GUARD FLUNG THE DOOR TO ANAIS' QUARTERS open. Part of her wished they would have put her in her former room, where she lived for so long. Instead, she ended up in a pantry closet converted into sleeping space with a small cot in it. She didn't dare leave the room while she'd been waiting. Instead, she'd tried meditating, praying like Drin so often did.

She found it hard to keep her thoughts on God. How did Drin manage to sit there for hours without his mind wandering or falling asleep? The Elorians made it look so easy. Her faith could never match theirs, could it?

It didn't matter now. The guard motioned her forward. "Come. Governor Jafil requires you."

She wasn't sure whether to dread speaking with the governor or to be hopeful. He seemed to want to earnestly consider her proposal, healing his son in exchange for letting her and Elaym go. She shouldn't hold out hope. The Sekaran's mind was drug-addled, at the very least. He couldn't be counted on for anything.

The guard led her through the kitchens, where Pyus were hard at work preparing meals for the Sekarans. Some glanced at her with curiosity as she still had no clothes on. It should have bothered her to be watched like that, but she felt no shame. The Sekarans had already taken everything from her. There was nothing left for her to lose.

They ended up in the main reception room, where the Sekaran governor lounged in a robe. Had he even moved from there in the several hours since she'd seen him?

Jafil stood, pipe in his hand. He appeared far more energetic than he had before and gave her a hearty wave. "Ah! Good. The Pyus girl. Welcome. I've been eagerly awaiting you for... Well, I don't have much of a sense of time anymore. All the days seem to flow together on this forsaken planet." He smacked his lips together. Then his eyes seemed to darken. "My son's health took a turn for the worse over the evening. I hope you're ready to uphold your end of the bargain."

Bargain? But they hadn't even agreed on anything. He'd said he would consider helping her. Did this mean he was going to go through with it?

Only one problem existed with her plan—her nanites were still inactive. She couldn't feel them. Would they come back to life when she needed them?

The governor hooked her arm and spun her around, dragging her with him up the stairs to the second floor, where she had lived before. They walked past her brother's room, her sister's. Finally they came to her own. Jafil released her and opened the door. His son was being put up in her room.

Anais closed her eyes to try to push back a flood of emotions from seeing her drapes, her furniture, her bed. She'd spent many nights going out to the balcony and looking at the stars, dreaming of being anywhere but this place. Now, she longed for the safety of those moments. The stars were filled with danger, not somewhere she wanted to be.

She opened her eyes again.

A Sekaran rested in her bed, under covers and hooked up to some medical machinery. Beads of sweat trickled down his face. His eyes were closed, but he still looked pained, tossing and turning in his unconscious state. Another Sekaran stood by him, looking at a datapad.

"This is my son's doctor, Metayin. Doctor, this Pyus woman claims she has the ability to heal my son. I command her to do so now."

Metayin looked at Anais skeptically.

"I..." Anais swallowed. "I'm going to need some time to assess the situation and make sure I understand your son's condition," she said. It was true enough. What she needed was to figure out how to get her nanites reactivated. Otherwise, she would be useless to the boy. "And I want to see Elaym before I do anything. Make sure he's unharmed."

Jafil clenched a fist. Anais recoiled, in case the governor decided to hit her. He opened his fist a moment later, drawing a deep breath. "Guard, go bring the prisoner here." He motioned to his son. "Assess away."

Anais moved to the bedside. She wasn't sure what to look for to even look like she was doing her part. She placed a hand on the Sekaran's forehead. It was balmy and hot. Definitely fevered, but Anais couldn't say what caused it. She was no doctor. The nanites healed as they willed, and she didn't understand their power or how it worked. She closed her eyes. *God, if you're there, please, help me. Repair the nanites inside of me. I need them now.*

Nothing.

"Do you wish to see the results of my tests?" Metayin asked.

Anais reopened her eyes. "Yes. Please." She should have thought of that first.

The doctor handed her the datapad. The text was in the Sekaran language and wouldn't be much good to her. Nor would the symbology or the charts of the boy's health. It all looked like gibberish to her. "I can't read this language."

"Of course not," Metayin said, his tone condescending. "The boy has been infected with bacteria from this world, and his system can't seem to fight it off. We don't have the proper immunities for whatever this is. Do you have a wonder-drug or some sort of antibiotic which will do the trick? I don't see anything on you." He motioned, referring to the fact she was unclothed, a slave.

Anais lifted her head, her ears standing erect atop her head. "I don't have that on me, but I won't need any drugs to do my healing when the time comes."

"The time is now!" Governor Jafil shouted. "You'll heal him now. If he dies—"

The guard returned. He was accompanied by a second guard as they each held Elaym by one arm.

Elaym's gray fur had been dirtied and singed, lacking the shining quality of a healthy Pyus. He'd paled. His face drooped, and he was so much skinnier than the last time Anais saw him. She could see his ribs through his fur, and he was completely unclothed, just like her.

The guards threw him to the ground in front of her.

"Elaym!" Anais cried, dropping to her knees in front of the other Pyus.

Elaym's eyes looked glassy, much like Jafil's had the night prior. "Is that really you? This isn't some kind of trick?"

"It's really me."

He scrambled backward. "I don't believe you. Anais is dead! They killed her. This is sick. I already told you. I don't have any more information. I've given you everything I have. Please..."

Anais placed a hand on his shoulder. "I was taken to another planet. I wasn't killed. I'm alive." Her heart sank in her chest as she realized what the implication of his words meant. Was her whole family gone? Did they kill them?

His eyes shifted. A hesitation. "Are you really?"

"I think that's enough for now," Jafil said, snapping his fingers. The guards grabbed Elaym by the arms and pulled him back to his feet, dragging him away from Anais.

Anais stood as Elaym disappeared from her sight. The governor pointed to his boy on the bed. "Heal the boy, and you can see your friend again."

She turned to the young boy, still tossing and turning on the bed, completely unaware of their presence. What could she do? She needed her nanites to work again before she could do anything. "I'm going to need some time," she said.

"You're not going to have time," Metayin said. "His condition's been weakening drastically. I doubt he'll survive another day."

Jafil stared at her expectantly. "You said you could heal him."

"I know..."

"No one lies to me." He smashed his fist against the wall. His fist made a dent in it, and he kept his hand clenched when he turned his attention back to Anais. He took a deep breath. "I'm sorry if that was unbecoming of me...my patience for falsehoods is very low. You didn't lie to me, did you now?" A sweet smile crossed his face.

This man was absolutely crazy. Anais had to remember that. And she had to be careful. "No, I didn't lie to you. It's just..." she moistened her lips. "It's a lot of pressure. I'm not sure I can do this with an audience."

Jafil frowned in consideration. Then he motioned to Metayin and his returning guards. "Out of the room."

"You can't be serious," Metayin said.

"I'm dead serious. This is my son's life."

"What if she harms him?" Metayin asked.

"What more harm could she possibly do? You said he might not last a day."

Metayin's face tightened, but he said nothing further.

"Come. We'll leave her be," Jafil said before flouncing to the door. Metayin followed him. The governor stopped, turning to look over his shoulder at Anais. "I'll give you three hours. If you fail, you will be executed." He didn't wait for Anais to reply before continuing out of the room and shutting the door behind him.

Anais stood in shock, alone in the room with the sick boy. The scene was oppressive. The air became stale soon after the governor had left.

What could she do? She had no way to heal him. Would escape be possible? She looked to the window. They were up on the second floor. It wouldn't be the worst drop to the first, but the odds of making it past the guards of the estate would be low. Every good option depended on having the nanites. "I don't suppose you can just beat this thing and get better?" she asked the sleeping boy.

He didn't answer her. Of course he didn't. He was comatose... or whatever state the sickness had him in.

The chrono ticked away on the wall. Fifteen minutes had already passed. Jafil had only given her three hours. What could she do? What would Drin do?

He'd pray.

Would that do any good here? Anais didn't feel comfortable in prayer, but she had nothing to lose by it, did she? Glancing around the room, she decided to sit down on the floor. She crossed her legs, just like Drin did when he went into his meditations, and placed her hands on her knees.

The foot of the bed was directly in her vision and distracted her, so she closed her eyes. The light from the room made the view behind her eyelids more of a light gray than black, but at least it was uniform. Anais took a deep breath.

*God, if you're there... I mean, I know you're there. I need your help. Make me like Drin. Help me with these machines inside of me. Get them going again.*

She thought the prayer to herself several times, not sure what else she should be saying or doing. She should probably ask for repentance for something or other, shouldn't she? Drin seemed to do that quite a bit. But what had she done wrong?

She could be brash sometimes, move a little too fast without thinking situations through. Were those sins? It didn't feel like it.

*Lust.*

The word popped into her head. It made her shift where she sat. Though she'd been the object of many Sekaran's lust, she hadn't done anything wrong. She'd done everything she could to spurn their advances.

It wasn't that. She was avoiding the problem. Her lust didn't have to do with any Sekarans, it had to do with Drin. Her throat constricted as she thought about it. This wasn't what she wanted to think about at all. She didn't have time for this. She loved Drin. Lust meant...

But she did want him physically as much as she yearned to be around him in other ways. Worse, she *knew* he had a vow of chastity. They could never be with each other that way, and yet she persisted with it. But what could she do about it?

Silence hung in front of her. No answer.

Anais clenched her teeth together, determined.

*Lord, forgive me for my lust for Drin and help me that I might not lead him astray.*

Thinking the words was like a weight lifted off her shoulders. It had been looming on her for days, weeks even. She loved him and wanted to be around him always, but she had to be cognizant that they could never have a relationship in the way she wanted. It hurt to think about, but admitting it to herself comforted her in some ways.

Warmth rose in her belly, filling her, circulating through her. She breathed in deeply to try to savor the moment. Was this God's forgiveness, His presence, his acceptance? The feeling Drin and

Jellal worked so hard to attain and remain in? No wonder they prayed so often.

She resumed her focus on the task at hand, praying for the ability to heal as she'd had before. She wanted to be like Marayh, strong enough to form an order of women healers around her. She'd never thought about what she wanted to do or be beyond liberating her people. Where did that come from? Was that God speaking her path to her?

Despite her attempts to remain focused, she found herself getting drowsy in the position. After a time, she dozed off.

She awoke to the sound of a door slamming open. "Well, you used your three hours resting up. Good, good. You should have the full energy to heal my son now," Governor Jafil said.

Anais took a moment to regain her surroundings, hazy from having just woken up. She stood and turned.

Jafil stood with Metayin and two of his guards. They didn't look like they had any sort of patience about them. Jafil rubbed his hands together. "Now what do you have?"

"I..." she didn't know what to say. She'd prayed, but then she fell asleep. How did she waste all that time? Was God even listening to her? She had no way of knowing. Every instinct in her told her to run, to try to push her way through the guards and make it out through the palace. She'd be faster than them, if they didn't gun her down.

But she didn't run. She turned to the bed instead, eyeing the boy with dread.

He lay still. Perhaps he no longer had the energy to toss and turn. His face was much paler than it had been before, his breaths shallow. The doctor may have been right in stating he didn't have long.

Anais made her way toward him, leaning over the bed. She pulled the sheets down to his waist, and then pressed her hands against his chest.

"What are you doing?" Metayin demanded. "This isn't a medical procedure. She's a witch!"

"Witch or not, I want her to try," Jafil said.

The pressure was on. Anais directed all of her will toward the boy. She didn't want to be distracted by the men behind her, taunting and goading as they were. She couldn't worry about Jafil's reaction if she failed. He would lose his mind on her, insane as he was. But it didn't matter. All that mattered was her. The boy. Her faith.

*Don't let me down,* she said to both herself and to God. A jolt ran up her spine like something had electrocuted her. Anais gasped.

Pink sparks shot from her hands and turned into a full glow. The energy brightened, swelling to encompass the space in front of her. The nanites had returned. The rush it gave her was like nothing she'd experienced before. Ecstatic, intoxicating. This was the will of God.

The nanites extended from her body, flowing into the boy and out again. They had a warming presence, making her feel whole again. It was like she'd been missing a crucial part of her existence since the Sekaran's grenade had detonated. Like she had been starved or parched. It didn't matter now. All was right in the world. The feeling lifted her to her toes, and she took it all in.

Several moments passed while the nanites did their work, cleansing the body of the boy. They flooded into her, and she stumbled backward. The rush was so much she could barely keep her footing.

Jafil steadied her. "That was an impressive display, but what did it do?" he asked.

Metayin brushed past them, tapping the display on the medical equipment. He shook his head several times. "I don't believe it."

"What?" Jafil asked. His slick fingers remained on Anais' arm and waist.

"His fever's gone. The bacterial infection levels appear to be at a low level."

"He's cured?"

"I wouldn't say all the way just yet, but enough of the bacteria's been killed that his immune system seems to be taking over and doing the rest of the work."

A wave of weariness overcame her. She could barely keep on her feet, even with the governor's help. "I need to rest," Anais said.

Jafil inclined his head toward the guards, who came to her side and relieved him of holding her up. "Put her back in her quarters."

"What about Elaym?" Anais asked.

Jafil didn't even turn to respond as she was ushered out the door.

# TWENTY-ONE

When Drin and his team returned to the airfield, they spotted a half-dozen Sekaran soldiers lingering around their shuttle. Two of the Sekarans searched the area while the others lounged about, not expecting any resistance. The mercenaries' advance scouts took cover around the corner of the former spaceport main terminal.

"We should be able to handle them, but we'll have to be careful," the mercenary team leader, Raydon, said.

Drin nodded. "I can head out and draw their fire. My nanites have restored."

"What if they have another one of the E.M.P. grenades?"

"I'll run back into cover. Hopefully you'll take out the bulk of them by then." Drin activated his armor, the full, gray-visored look of the intimidating Elorian Templar, and then allowed his light sword to form in his right hand. The few hours in which his nanites were deactivated had been torture. He was fortunate enough they had survived the EMP blast enough to bring themselves back to life. If he had no access to the nanites on this foreign world for his duration here, it could spell disaster for his team.

"Ready?" Drin asked.

The mercenaries shifted in unison, their weapons at the ready. They were disciplined, far better than he had envisioned mercenaries being when Anais's friend had first posed the idea of working with them.

Drin bent his knees and used his full nanite-driven momentum to boost him into the air. His entrance onto the runway would draw far more attention if he were dramatic. Which he didn't mind—the look of fear in the Sekaran soldiers' eyes when he descended upon them made it worth it.

Unlike the battle in the psychiatric ward, the enemy hadn't been prepared for an attack. The first two were still fumbling with their weapons when Drin sliced them in half in one stroke of his light sword.

The other four Sekarans scrambled to try to use the craft as cover, spreading out. The mercenaries fired their laser-repeaters toward the crowd. Several bolts dissipated into Drin's nanite shielding, but the others connected with two more of the Sekarans.

Drin leaped to the top of the craft, where he pivoted and descended on a shaking Sekaran, who reached for his comm unit. Drin drove his light sword right through the soldier, the comm unit rolling to the ground beside him.

No other Sekarans stood on this side of the craft, the right side if he were facing toward the cockpit. The remaining soldier must have been in the front.

Drin jogged in the enemy's direction, unafraid of the single soldier's ability to harm him. As he did, several more shots fired from the opposite side of the craft. By the time Drin rounded the corner, the Sekaran was down, shot with multiple laser bolts.

The mercenary team ran over to the craft. "Area clear," Raydon said.

"Good. Prepare the ship for launch, and let's find your fleet," Drin said. He glanced around at the mess, the six Sekaran bodies on the runway. Would it matter if someone else found them? It wouldn't if they didn't manage to bring the mercenary fleet for reinforcements. The Pyus would be stuck otherwise.

The mercenaries lowered the ramp. Drin entered the craft and made his way to the cockpit, assuming the main pilot seat where Jellal had been before. "Can any of you fly?" Drin asked.

"I can," Raydon said, taking the seat beside him.

Drin nodded to the competent mercenary team leader. He respected the man. If he could be converted to believe in the one true God, he would be quite the asset for the Elorians. But that would have to come later. They had a much more pressing task before them.

Raydon flipped the switches to power up the craft. The ramp raised and sealed. The other mercenaries strapped themselves in the back. Drin lifted them off quickly, taking a steep ascent. The g-forces keep him pushed back in his seat. He didn't dare linger, in case the Sekarans managed to get a signal out.

The ride through the atmosphere went quickly, the pull of gravity and acceleration becoming burdensome as they surpassed the clouds and reached escape velocity. Moments later, the craft's artificial gravity took over, and they entered into orbit around Pyus.

The spaceport looked so small from this height. The battles, the city—it was but a speck in the scheme of things. But even the small specks were important in God's creation. Drin kept a watchful eye out for any Sekaran craft, but none came. None of the orbital defense satellites activated for them, either. They were in the clear so far. Drin set a course for further out in the system, where, in theory, the mercenary fleet would be lying in wait. He relaxed as no hostiles showed up on the scanners. They'd made it. They would be in the clear of the Sekaran signal scattering field in minutes.

Drin turned back to check on the mercenaries in the back,

only to be met with the barrel of a laser-repeater to his face. He froze, but then inclined his head. "This is not a good idea," Drin said.

Raydon brandished a pistol from his co-piloting position. "Taking risks against the Sekarans isn't a good idea. You already lost your other Elorian friend. You know this is a fool's errand," he said.

"I go where the Lord takes me," Drin said.

The mercenaries laughed.

"Here's what we're going to do," Raydon said. "You're going to walk to the aft of the craft where there's an escape pod. We'll jettison you there and go back to our ship, tell Admiral Domen our mission was a failure, and move on with our lives."

Drin sighed. "Let's talk ab—"

"Now," Raydon said, grinding his teeth.

The confined quarters of the cockpit didn't make for a good place to make a stand. Drin pushed himself out of the area and moved toward the aft as Raydon commanded him. He didn't want to kill these mercenaries, or even harm them to any extent. Even though they were currently hostile to him, Drin needed them for the later assault. He had to be cautious here, and also careful not to allow them to blow holes in the craft by mistake.

One of the mercenaries pushed him.

Drin took a moment to regain his footing and then looked over his shoulder. What could he do? He spotted a gas grenade attached to the belts of one of the mercs. His nanite armor would protect him from the gas in all likelihood, and they'd be caught off guard.

With split-second precision, Drin ducked and reached for the grenade. He yanked it off the merc's belt. One of the others fired his laser-repeater, the bolt dissipating into Drin's shielding. He could take several more hits, even in close quarters.

"You idiots. Be careful about firing in the ship!" Raydon shouted.

It didn't matter. The mercs unloaded, but Drin was too quick for them. He dodged the first two bolts. The third hit his shield again. By that time, he'd removed the pin to the grenade and dropped it on the floor.

"Sleeping gas!" one of the mercs shouted.

"Hell," another said.

Gas flooded the compartment. The mercs tried to cover their mouths, but it only served to delay the inevitable.

Drin did his best to keep out of the way of any of the mercs who might get aggressive toward him. One charged him. Drin lowered his shoulder and rammed the merc in the gut, pushing him hard against the wall. His attacker succumbed to the gas a moment later, slumping to the floor.

Raydon was the last awake, having managed to get some cloth over his face. "You'll regret this!" he said, before wobbling and collapsing.

"I think not," Drin said, stepping over the bodies. He tapped the environmental controls to clear the gas and recycle the air in the shuttle.

Once back in the cockpit, Drin could see the main mercenary battleship up ahead, a small speck of light in the distance. They'd come up on them soon. He tried the comm.

The view of space shifted to the interior bridge of the starship. Admiral Domen's face appeared in front of him. "Elorian," he said. "Where are the others?"

Drin adjusted the view to the back of the craft to show the mercenaries, asleep on the floor.

"What did you do to my men?" Domen said, his face paling.

"They attempted a coup. I showed them why it's not wise to attack a Templar, even when outnumbering him."

Domen grumbled. "Raydon told me he didn't want any part of

this conflict between your religions. I didn't think he'd be so foolish."

"What's done is done. You owe Anais for the lives of your crewmen she healed. I have your scout team hostage. We need your help."

"Why don't you come aboard to discuss the situation?"

Drin shook his head. "I trusted the mercenaries enough already, and your people attempted to kill me. I'll keep your men safe, and you and I can talk from here."

Domen crossed his arm, but an expression of resignation crossed his face. "You don't give me much of a choice, Elorian. Give me your assessment of the world and what defenses they have, and we'll go from there."

# TWENTY-TWO

THE GUARDS ESCORTED ANAIS BACK TO THE LARGE FRONT sitting room. The fire was lit, leaving the room a warm temperature, which felt good on her face. She expected to find the governor inside. However, to her surprise, Elaym stood in front of the fire.

"You really are alive," Elaym said. He approached her, placing his hands on her shoulders, looking her over. "And very naked." He flushed, cheeks turning red even through his fur's coloration.

"It's not as if my fur doesn't provide cover. The Sekarans don't respect us. You get used to it," Anais said. She embraced him.

His modesty proved a little too much for the moment, and he kept her a short distance from him even in the hug, patting her on the back before moving away. "I knew there were some of us left alive," he said. "They kept trying to get information out of me. Asked me where people were hiding. I don't know anything. They grabbed me early on." He shook his head.

Elaym was nearly in hysterics. From what Anais saw of his interactions with the Sekarans, they hadn't been as kind to him as they were to her. She could only imagine the kinds of tortures they attempted to inflict upon him while he'd been caged.

"I'm sorry," Anais said.

"*I'm* sorry. I wish I would have been stronger," Elaym said, casting his eyes low.

"It's over now," Anais said. "Jafil told me if I healed his son, he'd let us go. That was the bargain I made."

"And you trust him?"

"Not as far as I can throw him, but I didn't have much of a choice," Anais said. She hoped the governor would honor his word. Even though he seemed to be crazy, he had a semblance of honesty to him.

Their conversation was cut short by the main doors opening, guards standing at attention as Jafil bounded inside. He took large steps but almost tripped over his own feet in the way he walked. His eyes were as glassy as they'd ever been, and his pipe hung from his mouth. Smoke rose from between his lips as he exhaled. He choked on the smoke, stopping to pull the pipe out of his mouth. Several coughs escaped him, and it looked like he might collapse to the floor from the fit.

The guards rushed forward to assist him, but Jafil waved them off. "Just a little smoke down the wrong pipe. You couldn't do much about it anyway." He cleared his throat. "Ah, my furred friends."

"I'm not your friend," Elaym said under his breath. It was quiet enough Jafil might not have heard him.

Anais turned and nudged Elaym with her elbow so he'd be quiet. She didn't need him harming any of the good will she'd earned for them. "Are you going to release us now?"

Jafil approached her, stopping dangerously close, his face inches from hers. He placed his pipe back in his mouth and blew smoke toward her face, making the air hazy between them.

Anais didn't flinch.

"I admire your tenacity, girl," Jafil said. "Most would have broken under the stress, but not you."

"I've lived through a lot."

"I can see that," he said, running the back of his fingers down her arm. He smacked his lips together. "You're a rather delightful specimen of your people. Has anyone ever told you that? I don't often find the lesser races attractive...but you..."

Anais held still, silent.

"Ah, well. With you being a slave, I suppose it takes the fun out of it. This whole world is so *boring*. I wish my betters would make up their minds as to what to do with it." He spun on his heels and took a few steps away from her. "But you did save my son's life, though. I owe you something."

"My freedom," Anais said.

"Ah." Jafil walked to the fireplace, holding his pipe away from him and flicking some of the ashes into the fire. "Yes, I know you desire your release. And also the release of your friend, who's been rather uncooperative in providing us good information in finding the insurgents." He turned back to her. "Perhaps you'd do better?"

Anais kept her expression flat.

"Or perhaps not." Jafil chuckled. "My guards wish to interrogate you, but I have the suspicion they wouldn't get much information out of you at all. It's too bad. Torture can be so much fun, but I'd hate to waste your life on a pointless endeavor." He paused, blinking. "Where was I?"

"Letting us go?" Anais asked in her sweetest tone.

"Ah. Yes. Letting you go. I do owe you, and yes, you and your friend are free to go. I must warn you, however, if you attempt to harm any of Eltu's chosen people on this planet again, your death will be excruciatingly painful, and it will not be swift. You will die begging for mercy from Eltu, and Eltu will not give it because you are an infidel."

Elaym started forward as if he were going to fight Jafil, but

Anais grabbed him by the wrist. "Not now," she said through her teeth.

"I suppose that is all. Thank you, sincerely for saving my son." As quickly as he had entered the room, the governor strode out of it, his guards moving behind him. The path to the front door was left clear for them.

"That's it?" Elaym asked, stunned.

"That's it," Anais said. "I wish he'd given me a cloak or something to wear. As much as I don't care what the Sekarans think of me, I'd like to maintain some sense of decency in front of *our* people."

"We can probably find something on the way out," Elaym said.

Anais nodded. They made their way into the residence's main entrance. Anais ran her hands along one of the columns. "I'll be back," she said to the house, her former home. It was stupid to talk to an object, but she missed the old days when she'd lived here in comfort, and she wanted to return under circumstances of her own choosing.

"Wait," Elaym said.

With no people around, the big entryway felt eerie. Anais didn't want to linger here any longer than was necessary. "What?"

"What if they bugged us. You know, to get the location of wherever our people are?"

"Right. Hold on..." Anais closed her eyes.

"What are you doing?"

"Quiet a second."

She focused on the nanites. They were there, alive, whole again. A gift from God. Life itself. They flared in activity when she thought of them, ready to obey her commands. In some ways, she was more connected to them than she'd ever been.

*Hello,* she thought to them, as if they were mini-people living inside of her. A tingling sensation ran up her neck. Were these tiny machines alive? Did they respond when she addressed them?

*Did the governor place anything inside of me? Tag me with something?* The nanites searched her.

"What's that light around you?" Elaym asked.

She didn't respond this time. She was too focused on everything in her. If they had placed a tracker in her, the nanites didn't find it. Anais opened her eyes, focusing on Elaym. The light flooded toward him.

Elaym backpedaled. "You're scaring me."

The nanite field surrounded him, despite his protests. He couldn't move out of their range while in this confined space. The nanites spotted something foreign inside of his body, electronic. A little chip someone had inserted into his forearm. The nanites found it, and they destroyed the technology.

Afterward, the nanites flooded back into her.

Anais gasped as she often did when the nanites rushed within her. She placed a hand on her chest. "Okay. We're safe now."

"How do you know?"

"You'll just have to trust me. Now, let's get out of here before they realize there's something wrong." She headed toward the big, arched front doorway, pulling it open. It was very heavy, but with the nanite assistance, she had little trouble at all. Everything was finally looking up. They passed through the doorway out into the cool outside air.

An explosion rocked the building.

# TWENTY-THREE

DRIN'S SHUTTLE REENTERED THE ORBIT OF PYUS, THIS TIME with a fleet of mercenary dropships behind him, along with a fighter escort. The fighters took care of the orbital defenses in no time. The automated defense systems were predictable, and the Sekarans had no preparations for an invasion fleet. The scattering field for communications held in place, however. Drin hoped it wouldn't prove to be a problem in the coming battle.

Twenty ships dropped into the atmosphere in unison, an impressive force. When Drin was with the Templars, he recalled missions where they would position themselves to blot out the sun before landing in order to intimidate their enemies. It wouldn't be a good idea here, as it would probably just panic the Pyus civilians. The locals had already faced enough problems with Sekarans slowing trade and slaughtering their nobility. God willing, life would be better for them again soon.

Drin muttered the Lord's prayer to himself.

Raydon glanced over from the co-pilot's chair. Even though they'd tried to mutiny, Drin allowed them to wake and retain their positions. Not without good reason. Before the assault began,

Raydon had had a long chat with Admiral Domen—perhaps chat wasn't the right word, as it was mostly the admiral chewing out the soldier. Even though it amused Drin, he sympathized with the mercenary. Raydon was now under pressure to perform or be faced with dismissal from the fleet. Loyalty to money cut both ways, Drin supposed.

Drin finished his prayer just as they descended through the clouds. The forested area of the capital had plumes of smoke rising from it. His internal warning sense went into overdrive. What had gone on when he was gone? He pushed the thrusters hard forward.

"Easy there. If we crash, we won't be able to help with whatever's going on," Raydon said.

"I won't crash," Drin said. He was a Templar. His reactions in piloting were superior to others', just as they were in all other regards. He couldn't voice the truth without causing strife, but he wasn't worried about losing control of the craft, even as he ripped through the sky with tremendous speed.

The other dropships did what they could to keep pace, but Drin pulled ahead of them. When he reached the treetops, laser-repeater fire shot in their direction, large bolts from stationary artillery in the forest below. "We've got incoming," Drin said.

"Assessing the trajectory and getting the coordinate information for our fighters," Raydon said. He moved like the wind to spot the location of their enemies—a small bunker just outside of the spaceport.

Two of the mercenary fighters broke formation with the fleet and came zooming past Drin's ship. They unleashed a barrage of missiles at the target, blowing it sky-high. The efficiency of Domen's men was impressive, to say the least.

"Good work," Drin said.

"I'll take that as a high compliment, Elorian. If they're firing anti-aircraft, they probably have troops waiting for us at the space-port as well. Is there an alternative point we can set down?"

Drin, looped the ship around, trying to find a place between the trees where they could make their landing along with the nineteen other ships behind them. "There's a clearing ahead," Drin said, pointing in front of him.

"It's going to be tight," Raydon said.

"I don't see any other options." Drin adjusted the controls to change the trajectory of the ship, and they sped to the point. It would set them back several kilometers. He hoped he wouldn't be too late to help Anais.

Turbulence rocked the ship. The winds made it difficult for Drin to set down with accuracy, but he would manage. This was no worse than several planets he'd dropped into before. He set down in the clearing, a hard landing that jolted the ship further. The mercs in the back complained, but there was little he could have done to land more smoothly.

The mercs were ready to go, combat armor on, rifles in hand. The ramp descended from the back. It was a good thing they'd been prepared for battle. Laser-repeater bolts slammed into the side of the dropship. The mercs stood off to the sides of the ramp, pointing their rifles out and firing blindly.

Drin rushed in front of the other mercenaries. He could absorb some of the fire and make it safe for the mercs to get out and take cover. Raydon barked orders for them to follow Drin's lead.

*Lord, give me the strength to do your will,* Drin prayed.

The mercs cleared the way for him, and Drin stepped out of the shuttle. He strafed, as to not make himself an easy target, even though some laser-repeater fire wasn't an immediate danger. If he took too many concentrated bursts, it could short out his nanites. He'd made the mistake of being overconfident and standing in front of fire in the past. Not this time.

Running forward, Drin activated his light sword. The mercs threw smoke grenades to add to the confusion of the situation. All the Sekarans would see would be the glowing light of his sword as it came down upon them. Divine wrath. The Glory of Yezuah.

A full squadron of Sekarans met them. Drin cut through several enemy soldiers, and yet they still kept coming from the trees beyond. They were everywhere. Laser-repeater bolts shot through the smoke. The pink shielding of his nanites activated to dissipate the blasts. Mercs fanned out behind Drin, firing their own lasers toward the incoming Sekaran targets. It was hard to move anywhere without running into laser fire.

As they fought, more mercenary dropships descended, filling the vacant areas of the field. One of the ships came too close to the trees on the opposite side, crashing into it, knocking one of the large trunks over as it collapsed further into the forest. Sekarans shouted, the poor piloting causing the tree to fall into the enemy lines.

*God always provides.* Drin grinned.

There were far too many of them, even for this much larger group of mercenaries. Drin and the scouts had underestimated the amount of Sekaran presence on the planet. The forest concealed too much, and their small force in the city proved to be an inaccurate representation of their prowess here.

Drin cut his way to the edge of the forest, where he grabbed one of the Sekarans by his battle armor and pulled the man toward him. The Sekaran's eyes went wide in fear, as most did when they faced a Templar. Despite being a soldier, the man shook.

"How did you know we were here?" Drin asked.

"We mobilized when we heard explosions in the city," the Sekaran said, shocked enough to respond.

"What explosions?"

"The local populace is terrorizing the governor."

Drin turned his head toward the city proper. Smoke covered the sky in the distance. The Pyus people must have made their move to fight back. But why now?

It came to Drin. Err-dio. His *squire* would have been a catalyst for action. It was bad timing, as Drin would have much rather the Sekarans surprised by their arrival. He hoped the Skree managed to rescue Anais from the Sekarans' clutches. If he had, Drin could focus on the battle and restoring this planet's order without worrying about her.

Anais occupied his mind far too much. "Is this your full force?" Drin asked, trying to stay focused on the battle at hand.

"I'm not answering your questions. Eltu will provide for me." The Sekaran lifted his head bravely, the shock of being drawn forward by a Templar wearing off. Every moment Drin didn't kill him, he would grow more defiant.

Drin jammed the light sword into the soldier's leg.

He howled. Another Sekaran turned and tried to tackle Drin from behind.

Drin kept facing his prisoner, bringing his light sword behind him. It ran through the attacking Sekaran soldier.

The action instilled the fear into the captured soldier. "You can't win. Our reinforcements are on the way. The fleet will be here before you can stop us. Eltu will save us!"

"There is no salvation in Eltu in this life or the next. I recommend you spend your last moments repenting and praying for Yezuah's forgiveness for your heresy," Drin said.

He lifted the Sekaran up and jammed his light sword into his chest.

The Sekaran gasped for air, choking as his lungs could no longer draw breath.

"God have mercy on your soul," Drin said, discarding the body.

If the Sekaran fleet was en route to the system, Drin needed to warn the mercenaries somehow. He had to find Raydon and get back with him. One of the ships could take off and get a message to Admiral Domen and prepare him.

Drin turned around, returning to the battle. The mercenaries continued to fire, hundreds of them scattered across the field, though the Sekarans still outnumbered them. Drin helped them to even the numbers. His light sword cut through Sekaran soldiers with very little resistance as he made his way back over to the dropship. He hoped he'd be able to find Raydon soon.

When he made it to the mercenary line, one of them saluted him. "Elorian," the mercenary said, with much more respect than they'd given him before. Funny how fighting side by side could instill camaraderie to people. They would come to understand the power of God.

"Have you seen Commander Raydon? I have an urgent message that needs to be delivered to the fleet."

"He's behind the dropship, directing the troops against the enemy."

Drin nodded to the soldier and then pushed past him. The Sekarans hurled a grenade into a group of mercenaries, causing them to scatter. Drin jumped to get out of the blast radius. It didn't detonate with any force, but could have been an EMP much like the one that short-circuited his nanites the last time. He didn't want to go through the experience again, especially not in the middle of this fray.

The fighting continued, Sekarans and mercenaries both scrambling for covered positions within the trees. It was becoming a mess to tell who was who, with all the smoke around. The lines became mixed. Guerrilla warfare.

Drin had his task, however, and wouldn't stop to get distracted by everything going on around him. He circled back to the dropship, where he found Raydon speaking into an earpiece with a datapad, plotting the coordinates of all of his men. "Ceres Five head west thirty degrees. You'll find their command group there," he said.

Drin waited until the man finished giving his orders before stepping into his field of vision to garner his attention.

"Elorian," Raydon said, looking up from his datapad.

"I have urgent information for you. Sekaran reinforcements are inbound. Someone needs to alert Admiral Domen," Drin said.

Raydon pressed a finger to his earpiece. "Fighter Squadron Rameses, do you copy? Are you still in range?"

Drin couldn't hear the conversation on the other end, but it appeared as if someone answered.

"I need you to take your group back to the fleet. Send them a message that the Sekarans are bringing reinforcements. No, we don't know how many. Tell Admiral Domen to expect inbound ships. Raydon out." He tapped the earpiece again. "I hope the information's enough, Elorian."

"I do as well," Drin said, turning his attention back to the battle.

"We're taking a lot of casualties. Domen thought this was going to be an easy assignment, open and shut. It doesn't appear to be the case."

"No, it doesn't," Drin said. He clutched his light sword more tightly, even though the nanites didn't require his holding them to stay active and flow as an extension of his arm. It felt natural to wield a sword the proper way. This battle would slow the enemy down for a while yet, and it was still in the opening volleys of this war for Pyus. "I'll see what I can do to even the odds."

Drin bent his knees, getting in position, and then he leaped, bounding through the air into the thick of the battle. His light sword would find the heads of many more blasphemers this day.

# TWENTY-FOUR

Smoke covered everything. Part of the front door had fallen on top of Anais, pinning her to the cold concrete at the front of her former residence. The blast made her ears ring. Her head pulsed as if she were trapped underwater and unable to hear anything but the ringing. It was bad enough as a Pyus, having sensitive hearing, but this was unbearable.

She writhed under the weight of the door, unable to get a glimpse of the rest of the front entrance from her position on her belly, facing toward the front gates. She hurt. Her ribs would bruise from colliding with the ground, and her back had never throbbed worse in her life. She clenched her teeth.

Elaym groaned from beside her.

It dawned upon her that she had more than her basic strength to rely upon in this situation. She had the nanites. They would help her. She just had to push aside all the discomfort and pain to focus for a few moments.

Elaym wouldn't have those abilities. He had to be in pain, which meant she had to make it right and help him. It was up to her.

Closing her eyes, she reached out to the microscopic machines living inside her. Healing would be helpful, but she needed more from them. She envisioned armor, like the kind Drin used to boost his strength. She hadn't used the nanites in that capacity since she'd first received them on Altequine, in the last battle there. Her effort saved both of their lives. What had she done then to make the nanites function in such a capacity? She breathed in and out and prayed. *God, if there's ever a time to help me, it's now.*

The armor formed around her. A hard shell, a small visor that gave her a projection from the nanites' viewpoint, helping her to see more clearly through the smoke and debris, along with so much more: heat, biosigns. With the armor formed, Anais effortlessly pushed the door off her, chucking it to the side. She lifted herself to her feet. The pain was gone now. Everything felt lighter. She glanced downward.

Elaym lay there, holding his head. "My ears," he muttered.

"I'm sorry," Anais said, crouching to offer him a hand. "I can take a look at them later if you're still having a problem."

"You... What are you wearing? Where did that armor come from?"

"It's a long story," Anais said. "But it's a helpful tool, and it's going to help us get out of here." She assisted him in getting up on his feet and looked past him. The blast had all but destroyed the front of her house. The whole face had collapsed. They'd been very lucky not to have more debris fall on them in the blast. If they'd stayed inside a moment longer, they wouldn't have lived to be viewing it.

Seeing her old home in shambles made Anais frown. This was the last of her old life. Her family had to be dead. She'd never be able to return to her room, to the comforts. When she was young, she used to sit on a blanket and slide down the stairs with her brothers. Her parents had yelled at her that they could crack their heads open, warning of the danger, but they still kept doing it. It had been too fun.

And now it was all gone. Rubble. Smoke covered everything. Embers and ashes fell.

It didn't matter. Houses they could rebuild. She needed to liberate the rest of her people from these Sekaran monsters.

"Do you think the governor made it out?" Elaym asked.

"I don't know, and don't much care. We need to get out of here before some of the soldiers come trying to find out what happened."

She led Elaym away from the building, prying open the maglocked gate with the raw strength of her nanites. They headed into the heart of the city.

Sekaran soldiers ran through the streets. It wasn't just small patrols like it had been before, but a whole force of them. They'd come out of nowhere...or they'd been stationed somewhere in the forests of Pyus. The problem with all of the foliage and trees covering everything was that it made it so easy to conceal a large force, something her planet had never had to deal with until now.

At least she knew the back alleys. Taking the main streets used to mean risking getting caught by someone who recognized her for being part of the Carver merchant lord family. She'd get caught for being out too late, clubbing with her friends. Those days seemed so much simpler, but they prepared her for this moment.

"This way," Anais said, veering off the main road and in between two trees where their trunks barely allowed for a person to slip through.

"Where are we going?" Elaym asked.

"A shortcut," Anais said. Easier than explaining how she wanted to avoid the possibility of running into any soldiers. She willed her nanite armor to dissipate and appear as normal clothing. The more they looked like two regular Pyus walking around, the less the odds they'd run into any problems.

"You're going to have to tell me how you change your clothes instantaneously like that," Elaym said.

"Faith," Anais said, bringing them into the denser areas of forest. It was dark there, difficult to see anything around them.

"This isn't a good area," Elaym said. "People used to sell dust here."

"I'm pretty sure they moved out in the open to get to that Sekaran governor," Anais said.

"Maybe," Elaym said.

They continued along a small dirt path. Several blasts echoed through the forest—more explosions—along with rapid laser-repeater fire. Something was happening, she just couldn't tell what.

The library loomed ahead of them, the building one of the few major landmarks still intact. It looked dead, no lights on inside. The large building represented the former glory of what Pyus had been. From there they turned back onto a larger paved street, coming up upon a crosswalk.

Laser fire erupted across the street from them, flying through the crosswalk. Anais couldn't see who was firing. She stopped in her tracks. "You should probably stay back," she said.

"What about you?" Elaym asked.

"I'll be fine." Anais took in a deep breath and reformed her armor.

She stepped forward into the crossroad. A signal for vehicles hung, suspended between tree branches. It had no power any longer. The streets were dead except for the fighting.

A cluster of Sekaran soldiers stood at one end of the perpendicular street to where she stood. They fired across and received fire from a group on the other side. Anais turned to look. They were Pyus, ten of them, all with Sekaran laser-repeaters in their hands. They were fighting back. Her people finally stopped cowering in their hollow trees and made a stand! Anais had never been so proud to be Pyus.

With them stood one person she recognized, a six-armed Skree. He held four different laser-repeaters, his middle arms steadying the upper and lower. The amount of firepower coming from him made him look like a hero out of stories.

The two sides fired multiple blasts at each other until one of the Sekarans pointed at Anais. "Elorian heretic!" he shouted.

"Drin?" Err-dio asked.

Everyone ceased fire in the confusion. Anais wasn't sure what to do. In the past, she would have run. This time, she chose to go forward instead of fleeing. She had the nanites—it was time to use them.

She sped into the line of Sekarans, though she'd forgotten to form a weapon to fight them. All the Sekaran guns trained on her. It would be fine, though. Her nanites would stop the laser-repeater fire from doing her damage, wouldn't it?

She focused, envisioning the light sword in her hand just like Drin used. The nanites formed the energy blade. She was getting the hang of her abilities, but she didn't know how to use a sword. Drin had such fluid movements in everything he did. It was like a brilliant dance when he went into battle. Anais flung her arms around, flailing them wildly. The Sekarans backed away from her, though none were hit by her work.

The weapons fire descended upon her. Anais was pounded by a dozen laser bolts. The blasts pushed her backward, causing her to lose her balance. Something flashed in her vision, red. A warning, but she couldn't read what it said because it was in the Elorian language. It couldn't be good.

Err-dio and the Pyus descended on the Sekarans to bring her back up. They fired on the enemy, picking off soldiers one by one. The Sekarans had ignored them to focus on Anais. Even as she fell to the ground, unable to stand through all the pressure of the laser-fire, many more Sekarans fell beside her. Her collapsing proved to be useful, as she no longer blocked the way of the laser bolts from her allies. They made quick work of the rest of the Sekarans, despite Anais' lack of fighting abilities.

Err-dio rushed to Anais. "Drin! Are you okay?"

"I'm not Drin," Anais said.

"Anais?" Err-dio laughed and helped her to her feet. "I saw the armor..."

"I've been in armor before," she said. The world wobbled, making it difficult for her to stay on her feet. The nanites had lost their bearings under all the fire, but she understood they were repairing themselves. She could feel them replicating inside of her, tiny shocks of energy pinching through her system. "What's going on?"

"When Drin left, some of your friends were getting antsy. They wanted to make a move, so we decided to try to liberate you from the governor's palace. It worked?" Err-dio smiled.

Elaym moved over to the other Pyus to talk to them.

"He released me," Anais said.

His smile faded. "Oh. I thought we'd accomplished something. We got the Sekarans out of their hiding, though. There's a lot more of them than I thought there were on this planet."

"I think we're all surprised by their numbers," Anais said. "So, now what? We have to regain control over the city somehow."

"We're doing what we can to do. I've gathered up as many of your compatriots as possible and broken them into units. A lot like Drin did for my people when he came to my world. Because your species has natural speed, they're better geared for hit and run missions. Like the one at the governor's mansion. We're all working on regrouping and figuring out the next target to make it easier for the mercenaries when...if they arrive."

*If* they arrived. Anais looked up to the sky. It looked like there were several ships descending in the distance. Were they mercenaries or Sekarans? Before Anais could reply, one of the Pyus shouted, "We have incoming!"

More Sekaran soldiers, a dozen at least, flooded into the streets from two different directions. "Get your men back," Anais said.

Err-dio nodded, trusting her far too much. What did she know about battle? The Skree retreated along with the other Pyus. As soon as the Sekarans came into range, they began opening fire. The street turned into complete mayhem. Anais could barely see through the laser bolts. But she could still move quickly.

She zigged and zagged through parked vehicles, making it difficult for the Sekarans to target her. Because of the sheer number of soldiers, some of the laser bolts hit Anais' shielding, but her nanites had managed to repair the worst of the damage from the prior assault. They worked quickly inside her, fueling her with more energy than before. Was this how Drin managed to stay fresh through endless battles? Anais came upon the Sekaran lines. She still wasn't the best with wielding her light sword, but this time she managed to strike true. The blow caused the lead Sekaran to fall and knock over two of his fellow soldiers. They all focused on her now, but in close range.

The Sekarans pushed her back against a storefront from their blasts. Anais fell backward through a window, which shattered all around her. The armor protected her skin from what would have been thousands of tiny cuts otherwise. But now she was trapped in a place she couldn't escape for the fire. More than a dozen Sekarans faced her as even more rushed down the street toward the others. Her friends didn't have enough support, and she wasn't going to be much help to them. What could she do?

She pushed herself to her feet again, clutching her light sword in her hand.

All of the laser-repeater fire came slamming into her then. Bolt after bolt pounded at her shields. Every step forward was met with energy force pushing her feet back. Eventually, her foot backed against a pony wall, stabilizing her, but she couldn't move under all the fire. Her visor flashed red warnings again, which she now knew to be a sign of the nanite fields losing their integrity. It was too much. She'd failed.

*God, forgive me,* Anais prayed. *I know I rush into things, it's my weakness. I just wanted to save my people. Please protect them, even when I'm gone.*

The world began to swirl. Everything became so hazy she could hardly see. The laser-repeater fire kept bombarding her.

A large shadow descended on the Sekarans. Something was coming down from above. Was it a big ship? In the middle of the city? Some of the Sekarans diverted their attention, but not enough of them. Anais fell to her knees. Tears streaked down her face. The bolts penetrated the shielding, hitting her armor. Each hit felt like a punch to the gut, and it would be even worse when the armor failed.

A bright light shone in front of her as she lost consciousness.

# TWENTY-FIVE

In many ways, fighting through the streets of the city was easier than in the clearing. It provided a confined area so the Sekarans couldn't spread out and come at Drin from too many multiple points. They were confined by the large trees and buildings here. He could systematically work his way through their lines. With the mercenaries at his back, they found their way about halfway into the city before too long.

The mercs didn't have the benefits of the nanites, either the level of the added strength or the extra energy they gave to keep him fighting through all of the fatigue that came with battle. The others needed to take brief breaks in between skirmishes, which Drin allowed and slowed himself for, but they needed to keep pushing as fast as possible. "Come on. This planet might depend on us establishing a foothold in time," Drin said.

They'd just made their next push into the streets when Drin saw the Sekarans were faced the opposite direction. They focused their fire into a building with blown windows. It made for easy targets.

Drin rushed ahead of the mercenaries and jumped to a

balcony on a branch about one story up. From there, he swung from the branch, bringing his light sword up over his head, and descending into a pack of Sekarans at the front of the building. He stabbed through three of them before he landed and turned to cut through another. Others fell from the blasts of laser repeaters from Drin's allies.

By the time the Sekarans figured out what was happening, only two remained standing. One began to flee, but directly into the group of mercenaries at Drin's back. He didn't worry about the runner but faced the final Sekaran still facing him. "Repent," Drin said.

"Never. I will go to the afterlife and receive my rewards."

"So be it," Drin said before running his light sword through the Sekaran's chest.

Drin took a deep breath, taking advantage of the lull in the battle. He could relax, at least to some extent. No enemies stood in front of him, though there would still be many up ahead. He turned toward the broken window in the storefront, seeing motion inside. He held his light sword up, which helped to illuminate the inside of the store. And there he saw the gray armor, lights flickering on it. Elorian Templar armor. Smoke wafted from it. The person inside wasn't moving.

*Anais.*

He rushed forward, stepping over the sill and ignoring the shattered glass all around him. The place was dark, and Anais writhed on the ground. At least the armor was still active. It meant the nanites hadn't completely shorted out.

Drin dropped to his knees in front of the girl, unlatching the nanite-composed helmet from her head and setting it to the side. Ordinarily, the helmet would have dissipated, but with her in such dire straights, her armor remained to protect her. He placed his fingers in front of her lips. She still breathed, but very shallowly.

Closing his eyes, Drin focused on his nanites. They flowed

inside of him. His gifts were not in healing, but he could do some modest work. If her own nanites were still active, his could interact with hers.

Even through closed eyelids, intense pink light filled his vision. He could feel her life force. Erratic. Bouncy, even in her incapacitated stated. Her world was filled with optimism and joy he didn't share, but he wished he could. He longed for it in many ways, and the connection with her nanites, with her essence, brought him a sense of peace he hadn't found in a long time.

It was taboo to connect like this except in life-threatening situations. Though why should it be? Why shouldn't the Templars share greater bonds between the blessed technology that flowed through each other and better know each other's souls? In Heaven, they would have a shared worship in unison. This was the closest thing to what Heaven must be like.

His nanites made their repairs, jumpstarting the process of self-replication, healing her.

Anais gasped.

Drin opened his eyes. Anais' big eyes stared directly at him, longing, searing through to his soul.

"An angel," Anais said.

"Hardly," Drin said. He offered his hand to her. "Are you able to sit up?"

"I think so," Anais said. "My head feels like I drank far too much liquor."

"It's the healing process. You'll be fine in a few minutes. Try to coax the nanites into restoring your energy. We have a lot of fighting left ahead of us," Drin said.

She looked so innocent. Not the type who should be involved in this kind of battle. It was unfair that she'd been left at the mercy of the Sekarans. But God had a plan, and she was a big part of it.

"Did the mercenaries come?" Anais asked, pushing herself to her feet.

"They did. They're with me," Drin said. He pointed outside the window to where Raydon and a large contingent of his men stood at the ready, awaiting further orders.

"Then we have a chance," Anais said.

"We do, but there's far more Sekarans here on the planet than we planned for. I believe they had their bases within the trees outside the city so they didn't have a disrupting presence. Your people didn't have good information on them, and we weren't able to obtain any, either. I've sent word back to Admiral Domen. He needs to send more men if we're going to survive this. And we have to find the comm scattering field and make sure to take it out of operation."

"Where do we start?" Anais said.

Drin stood, leading her out of the storefront. "Once we have control of the city, we'll have a better idea. For now, we need to clear the streets and establish a central command."

"The library," Anais said.

"Hmm?"

"The library will work great as a command. They have full access to the nets, large open spaces, and, uh, I think it's pretty defensible. It has good lookout points that allow people inside a view of the city. We'll be able to see any Sekarans coming," Anais braced herself on Drin's arm as she stepped over the window sill.

Drin followed after her. "Let's head to this library then."

Raydon inclined his head toward Drin and Anais. "The woman has Templar armor? I thought only Elorians had access to your strange technology."

"It's a long story," Drin said.

Raydon shrugged. "The men are ready. Thank you for giving us another break so soon after the last one."

"We're going to head to the city library and establish a base there. Then we need to figure out where the scattering field is coming from so we can contact your fleet at will." And perhaps call for some Templar back up. If they were going to secure this system long-term, they would need more than just the mercenaries' help.

The group continued down the city street, with Anais taking the lead so she could show them the way to the library. So many dead lined the sidewalks, mostly Sekaran. Anais must have fought her way through the opposite way, but there were Pyus fallen amongst the dead enemies. The populace had put up at least some resistance.

They turned a corner, and laser fire erupted. Drin and the others rushed back to use the building as cover. From further down, he heard shouting.

"Hold your fire!" someone said. "Friends! I'm going to round the corner. Don't shoot!"

Drin held a hand up to tell the mercenaries to hold. They were well-disciplined, and he didn't worry about them following orders too much. A figure rounded the corner, one with three arms on each side of his body. Err-dio.

"Squire," Drin said, grinning with amusement.

Err-dio beamed at the title. "Templar Drin," he said. "I'm very glad to see you. We've cleared most of this area of the Sekaran threat, and Krytien believes he knows where the comm scattering field is coming from. We were about to head to the city's central power station to take it down."

The central power station. Drin considered. It would be better to remove the scattering field first before accessing this world's nets from the library. "New plan," he said to the mercenaries. "We'll take out the central power station first, then we'll come back to the library to establish command."

"Won't it shut down the power to the library?" Err-dio said.

"My men have portable generators if there's an issue. I can send some of them to the library in advance if you'd like," Raydon said.

Drin shook his head. "We shouldn't split our forces just yet. I don't trust that the Sekarans don't have an overwhelming force nearby. But let's hurry. Lead the way."

Err-dio whistled his people over. More than fifty Pyus stood with him, all carrying Sekaran laser-repeaters. Krytien stepped forward. "Let's go. Hopefully, you can keep up with us," he said, a knowing smile crossing his face.

The Pyus could move fast, but the mercenaries were trained soldiers, and Drin had the assistance of the nanites. Everyone managed to stay together as they rushed through the war zone. On their way to the power station, they came across a few rogue Sekarans, who had survived prior encounters, and dealt with them accordingly. No large force met them in the city streets. They'd been blessed so far.

The power station came into view, a large, chain-link fence around it with electrified wire up top. The mercenaries rolled a grenade at the fence, blowing it to pieces. The fence flickered and sparked, but they had their way in.

The station was a cylindrical building with two flatter buildings on either side. Trees were cleared around it, unlike most Pyus establishments. It made sense, since the trees could catch fire if there were an issue with the electrical station.

Again, they found no Sekaran resistance as they moved inside. The place was eerily quiet. The hum of electricity ran throughout the place, but little else. Krytien did most of the searching of the place, understanding the Pyus language and the set-up of the power structure. Eventually, he led them to an area out back of the main cylinder. It was cordoned off with another fence and had signs which appeared to be warnings.

"Here it is," Krytien said. "The main transformer. If there's a scattering field using city power, it'll go down when we take it out here."

Raydon motioned to the mercenaries. "Set your charges, then let's get a safe distance away."

His men went to work, placing three different explosives from their packs on the transformer and securing them to it. The mercs were prepared for all sorts of different scenarios. They were a blessing. Despite the earlier mutiny attempt, Drin was glad to have them with him.

They backed out of the power plant to the front and outside the main electrified fence. Then the mercenaries who had set the charges clicked their detonators.

The power plant went up in a massive explosion. It rocked them even from outside of it, shaking the ground. Nearby tree branches swayed, some cracked and fell. A plume of smoke shot into the air. The charges didn't set the whole place into an explosion, however. The main cylinder where the fusion power was created was built to handle outside forces. The transformer explosion proved enough to take out the electricity in the city. Lights turned off everywhere. The electrical hum of the fence stopped. Everything went quiet.

"We did it," Raydon said, tapping his datapad. "The scattering field is down. I have connection with the fleet."

"Great," Drin said. "We might have a chance after all."

Anais pointed to the sky. "Is that them? The main ships are landing!"

Drin looked up. It was evening. The stars and moons lit the sky well-enough. Then, a long, ominous shape blotted out the sky, obscuring the stars above them. Dread crept through Drin's spine, causing him to shiver. He recognized the sight of that ship, and then five more as they drifted in the sky.

The Sekaran fleet had arrived.

# TWENTY-SIX

Fire rained from the sky. The Sekarans responded to the Pyus insurgence with a full-scale assault on the planet. Laser beams the size of buildings cut through everything. One of the larger trees split down the middle, crackling and booming as the lasers hit, becoming smoldering firewood.

The population panicked. Pyus civilians ran through the streets haphazardly, creating even more chaos. Someone had to get them under control, but how? Anais didn't even know where to begin. She looked to Drin for guidance.

The Elorian still had his Templar helmet covering his face. She couldn't read his expression, but she could reach out with her nanites. Their two fields of energies interacted. Anais caught a glimpse of his thoughts. He was praying. Of course. Through everything, Drin held steadfast in his faith. He asked God what to do.

*Well, God, what do you want me to do?*

She was answered by another burst of laser fire, penetrating the street ahead of her. Chunks of asphalt shot into the air. Pebbles came flying toward her. Anais' armor and shielding blocked most of the debris, but the main laser fire was steadily coming her direction.

"Get out of the way!" Anais shouted to several of her fellow Pyus.

The civilians didn't hear the warning in time. The Sekaran ship lasers overpowered them. The biological forms disintegrated into nothingness before Anais' eyes. Her people. She wanted to vomit.

Her reaction caused her to freeze in the middle of the street, right in the path of the laser. In her case, she was fortunate to be connected with Drin. He moved like the wind, sweeping her into his arms and carrying her away. He took a big leap, dashing them through the air. The laser beam cut through the street, hitting where Anais had been standing. Without Drin's exceptional abilities, she would have never made it out of the way in time.

Dozens of fighters flew overhead, combing through and using their smaller lasers and missiles to destroy what the larger battleship missed with its wide beam. It was a carpet bombing. They were going to flatten this city, and Anais was helpless to do anything about it.

Drin led her by the arm, carrying her to the shelter of a metal structure that survived the blast. He stayed under an overhang with her.

"Where are the others?" Anais asked.

"I don't know. I didn't have time to check to see where they were going *and* get you out of the way," Drin said.

Anais's shoulders slumped. It was all her fault. Everything she did caused problems for Drin and his plans.

"You didn't do anything wrong," Drin said, as if sensing her thoughts. He may have sensed them in earnest, if their nanites were still interacting. "The Sekaran fleet arriving is an unfortunate turn of events. We're going to have to improvise."

Ships zoomed above, creating a sonic boom above them that

*cracked* in the air. Anais peeked her head outside the overhang to look up. The mercenary fleet was in the air. Their fighters tangled with the Sekarans'. The lasers no longer fired toward the ground but at other ships. The sky lit up like fireworks.

Drin joined her in staring up at the sky. "At least the fleet kept their word. Perhaps all isn't lost, though I'm not sure the mercenaries can handle the full might of the Sekarans. We should proceed to the library like originally planned. If it's still standing, we can establish a ground base to try to regain control of the situation here."

"What about all of the civilians?" Anais asked.

"Unless there's a way to send messages to them to calm down, clear the streets, and return to their homes, I'm not sure there's much we can do for them. It's going to be some time before we restore order," Drin said. "Lead the way?"

Anais nodded. Her mind reeled. So much destruction in so short a time, she could hardly focus on the task at hand. But Drin remained calm and stoic, as if this were an ordinary situation. How did he do that? Sensing his strength through the nanites helped firm her resolve. She could do this. If only to make it to the library. Anais stepped out of the cover of the structure and moved down the street.

Devastation lay everywhere she looked. The whole city caught flame from the laser fire. No one worked to put it out. Smoke covered everything. Her nanites filtered the air through her mask, but she could only imagine how difficult it would be to breathe otherwise. With the transformer down, no other lights shone in the city. They didn't need to with the bright laser fire overhead. The light came in bursts, but Anais' visor shifted into a night vision setting, allowing her to see without any issues.

They passed several scared Pyus, hunkering under various shop overhangs, trees, and in the door frames of various buildings. They all seemed so scared, and they looked at Anais and Drin with equal amount of fear. They had no way of knowing Anais was one of them and here to help.

A child screamed in the doorway of one of the buildings they passed. His mother clutched him to her chest. "No, no, no!" the mother shouted.

Anais put a hand out to stop Drin. "We have to help them," she said.

"We'll help them best by establishing command and securing the city," Drin said.

Anais turned to him. "Did the Lord Yezuah have compassion on the injured and sick, or did He stick to his mission?"

Drin held silent. Lasers crackled in the distance. "The Lord put you here to remind you of my failings." He motioned her to head over to the family in the doorway.

Anais nodded to herself and moved to them. The woman was on the ground, so Anais crouched.

The woman looked at Anais in fear. "What do you want?"

"Oh," Anais said. She let the helmet around her dissipate. The sudden rush of the smoke-filled air made her cough and her eyes water. She covered her cough with her mouth. "Sorry. I want to help your son. What happened?"

"The lasers came out of the sky. We were just walking in the streets. I don't know what's happening. Everything was fine, but, today, the soldiers and all of the fighting... I just want everything back to normal again." The woman sobbed. "My little Meeks will never be normal again."

"He might be. Can I see him?" Anais asked. Her whole chest tightened at listening to the woman. This war hurt the regular people. Anais doubted herself, this mission, whether they were doing the right thing. But she had seen firsthand how the Sekarans brought pain and destruction wherever they went. She couldn't lose faith, not now.

The woman held the boy out toward her. Dried blood caked

his fur all over his face and upper body. At his chest and shoulder, all of his fur had been burned off. Pus and ooze seeped from the wound. It looked infected.

It wouldn't be a problem. Anais breathed in slowly, letting the nanites flow through her. She'd done this before and could do it again. *God, let me help this little boy,* she prayed. The nanites reacted in their same familiar way. They vibrated, almost like they had their own feelings and were exuberant to be used. This was what they were instilled into her for. Her purpose. She would heal those who were suffering.

The nanites' light burst from her like an exploding star. The woman covered her face. It didn't take much time. The nanites stitched up the wounds, cleaned up the boy, and healed him. His fur even returned where he'd been struck by the laser fire.

Anais lost her balance in her crouching position, but Drin was there to catch her. She looked up at him and smiled. "Thank you," she said.

The woman burst into tears as she clutched her boy even closer to her. "No, thank you. I can't believe it. It's a miracle!"

"Go and tell everyone you know that Yezuah is real, and He heals those who needs it. He is the one true God," Drin said.

The woman looked to Anais as if trying to verify.

"He's right," Anais said, letting Drin help her to her feet.

"I'll tell everyone, I promise!" the woman said.

"Mom?" the boy asked weakly. He looked at his mother curiously. The woman squeezed him again.

"We should go," Drin said.

Anais nodded, reformed her helmet and visor, and turned. She'd done what she'd set out to do on a small scale, now it was time to save her whole world.

Even though the act of healing someone took a lot out of her, she was instilled with a sense of energy from the woman's reaction. She could make a difference, even if it was a small one. Not everything she did was a problem. That was only her doubt talking when she'd thought those terrible things.

They continued down the street, having to detour around an area engulfed in flames. Anais could feel the heat from the flames as they approached. "Will the nanites protect us from fire?" she asked.

"To some extent," Drin said, "but we shouldn't test our limits. The Lord is clear He should never be tested for the sake of it."

They looped around another street. During their walk, the battle above seemed to come to a halt. There were a lot fewer ships in the air. None of them appeared to be from the mercenary fleet. The long, needle-like fighters the Sekarans flew looped around the city. Had the mercenaries lost? There had to be more ships than that. Didn't Domen tell them they had more? Anais hoped it wouldn't be the only help they'd receive.

They came toward the library from the south side. Anais let out a sigh of relief to see the building still stood completely intact. How the Sekarans' fire had missed the library was beyond her, but it had happened. She quickened in her pace, excited to make some headway toward freeing her people.

The library was dark compared to the burning city, and without the firefight in the sky, it would have been hard to see, without the nanites' help. She stopped in her tracks, realizing she'd been jogging, getting ahead of Drin.

"One thing you'll need to learn in your journey is patience," Drin said.

"One thing you'll need to learn is how to not be rude!" Anais replied, spinning and finding herself smiling at him. Despite every-thing around them, Anais was glad she had Drin by her side. Even if it couldn't be in the way she desired him, it felt right to be with him.

Her brief moment of levity was interrupted by several flash-lights rounding the library from the west. She spun around again, facing toward them. The lights shone in her eyes, and the soldiers holding them shouted in the Sekaran language. Her visor translated it as, "The infidels! Kill them for Eltu!"

She could tell by the light radiating from behind her that Drin had activated his light sword. Anais scrunched her nose to focus and did the same. More soldiers to handle. She was beginning to get the hang of this. Anais was about to charge but stopped herself when she saw two Sekaran men pressing through the group of soldiers.

They had prosthetic arms made of metal and another modification to their skulls, a computerized block that connected to a green visor over their beady red eyes. These weren't ordinary soldiers, they were battle mages. The last time Anais and Drin faced just one of them, they'd almost been killed. Now they would have to face two.

# TWENTY-SEVEN

"Stand back!" Drin shouted. He hated yelling at Anais like this, but he couldn't spend time mincing words in the heart of battle.

She stood in front of him, backtracking toward him, her light sword in hand.

The Sekarans moved with speed and precision. The battlemages shouted, directing their people to open fire. Laser-repeater shots came toward them. Drin had to move forward quickly so they wouldn't get trapped.

He burst toward the battlemages, ignoring the other soldiers. They wouldn't be able to fire at him when he was in close range to their leaders. He pushed his light sword toward the leftmost battlemage, but the man held both hands up, wrists together. It created a bubble, an energy dead zone where the tip of Drin's light sword dissipated.

The second battlemage shot a wave of energy at Drin, pushing him to the side. His feet slid across the cobbles, but he managed to keep his footing. As he did, he cut through two of the Sekaran soldiers. Several laser bolts pounded into him, but Drin pressed forward again.

Anais hadn't listened. She'd circled around to the back, catching the Sekaran soldiers off guard. She took out one who didn't see her, and another as he turned around to fight her.

"Get out of here!" Drin shouted.

"I'm not abandoning you!" she yelled back.

Stupid woman. Drin clenched his teeth together as he charged the battlemages again. He couldn't afford to ignore them even for a second. He drove his light sword at the same battlemage, prepared for the tip of it to dissipate. Drin used the distraction to deliver the battlemage a kick to the gut, throwing him off balance and turning him around. The second battlemage yelled to try to get Drin's attention, but Drin saw the opening and stayed focused on his one target.

His sword reformed, and he pushed it upward, toward the battlemage's skull, right at the rectangular protrusion, which contained technological components that allowed the battlemages their power. If he struck true...

Drin thought he'd missed. The battlemage jerked his head, making the strike all but impossible to hit. Drin managed to contort at the last moment. The benefits of having a light sword instead of a real one, was the strength didn't matter with the blow as much as the precision of where it hit.

The move worked. His blade drove directly into the circuitry, sparking when it hit. The battlemage gasped, caught off guard by the sudden movement. He started to convulse, his lip quivering and eyes rolling back.

The second battlemage cried out, a guttural noise that caused Drin to flinch. The brief moment of lack of focus was enough for his enemy to strike. Drin turned, but the battlemage held a large orb of energy between his hands. The orb shot forward, blasting through Drin's shielding and into his chest. The force was enough to push Drin end over end. He flipped backward, drawing himself into a ball so he could tumble and not hit his head. Even through the armor, landing hard on the spine took its toll. Pain reverberated through his body. He tried to right himself.

Another orb flew at him.

He braced for getting hit hard again, but this one didn't land. It pushed hard into a shield and the energy shot to the sides. Drin looked up.

Anais stood behind him, holding out her hands, creating a stronger shield barrier out of the nanites than was typical. All of her energy appeared focused into it. "Get up!" she said.

Drin scrambled to his feet. As much as he'd been chastising her for being foolish earlier, he felt bad about it now. Without her, he probably would have been killed by the second blast, or at least incapacitated so another one could finish him. But instead, he rose to put up another fight.

He still couldn't trust that this battlemage would make the error the last one had. This one appeared to be smarter, standing back, away from Drin, shuffling so that he always kept Drin within his line of sight.

Without the risk of hitting their leaders, the Sekaran soldiers reopened fire. The blasts hit Anais's super-shield. It began to sputter. "I can't hold it for much longer," Anais said.

Drin lowered his voice. "We make a break for it. Inside. We'll have better odds if they can't stand out in the open and fire at us."

"Got it." Anais said as more laser bolts pelted.

The remaining battlemage gathered his energy again. Anais dropped her shield and took off running.

Drin followed. When the Pyus woman was at full speed, she raced faster than he did. He kept up, barely. She didn't bother to open the glass doors to the library, bursting through and shattering them. Drin darted through the aperture after her.

Soon, they were deep inside the dark building. It was held up by the trees of the forest, and large cabinets full of books stood as far as Drin could see, with a large dome that opened into the forest, allowing the moonlight to shine down into it. No other light came through, the city's power still down.

Drin slipped past Anais to lead her into the long rows of books. He didn't know his way around the library, but he didn't need to learn the ins and outs of the building's layout. All he had to do was slow the Sekarans down while they regrouped. He turned once in the middle of the room, and pushed a couple of the cabinets over. Books scattered everywhere, an effective barrier made.

"What are you doing?" Anais asked.

"Buying us time." Drin looked around the library. They needed to do more to fortify their positions. He'd been able to take out the first one by sheer luck. This battlemage would be able to blast through all of this stuff easily. How could they stop him?

Footsteps crashed on glass. Sekarans barked at each other in their language. They were coming. "We can bring the place down on them," Drin said to himself.

"What?" Anais whispered.

"If we cut out the support trees, we can trap them in here. Collapse the building."

"We can't do that!"

"Why?"

"It's the library. We need it."

"You won't need anything if the battlemage keeps roaming free. You'll be dead." Drin said.

Anais grimaced.

"Here's what we'll do," Drin said. "You'll go to the back tree there," he pointed, "and then use your nanites to cut through the trunk. I'll do the same at the front, and we'll destabilize one side of the building. It should all come crashing."

"I really don't like this," Anais said.

"We have to move quickly. Go." Drin didn't waste any more time arguing. He never had to deal with that with his men in the Templars nor with the mercenaries. The benefits of trained military life.

Drin kept his focus ahead. He relied on Anais to follow orders, even though she had a track record of *never* listening to him. He hopped over the books spilled on the floor, making his way through the aisles to the side of the building.

The Sekarans had split up and spread out around the large room. Two soldiers stood in front of Drin when he turned and headed to the front-right tree column. He rushed forward, forming his light sword. The Sekarans each managed to get their shots off, easy for Drin's nanite shielding to handle, but the problem was, it would alert the others. Drin pulled his blade for a wide slice, lobbing off the soldiers' heads in one blow.

He didn't have time to stop and admire his handiwork. The other Sekarans would be on him soon, and he had to complete the mission and get out of here. He concentrated his energy on his speed, hurdling over the bodies in front of him to make it to the wide-tree column that held the building up.

His light sword would be too thin to do much here, so he let it dissipate. Would Anais be able to use her technology similarly? He focused, creating a sheet of nanites between his hands, which he held out. Planting his feet, he forced that energy forward.

It cut through the tree as if it were paper. The trunk crackled and rumbled. Drin drew the energy up to create a bigger hole in the trunk and really collapse it. The area Drin cut turned into dust. He could smell the scent of freshly cut tree even through his mask.

Laser bolts hit him from behind. He was out of time. Drin didn't wait for his handiwork but let the nanites dissipate and took off running toward Anais. The Sekarans turned the corner, firing in his direction.

Anais struggled with the tree ahead. She had her normal light blade formed, not having learned the trick Drin created to cut through it. She was going to slow them down. Laser bolts followed Drin, blowing past his head as he hurried toward her. "Out of the way!" He said.

He pushed Anais to the side, forming the sheet of energy in front of him as he had before, pushing it into the tree. He let the nanites evaporate right away and formed a new blade, cutting through the wall to the side.

"I'm sorry," Anais said.

Drin grabbed her by the wrist and pulled her through the hole. The crackling started. With two of the pillars of the building now unstable, it began to rumble. The Sekarans weren't prepared for the collapse, just as Drin had hoped. He glanced back to see the Sekarans readying to fire at him and Anais, now outside of the library and in the streets. The battlemage walked up behind the Sekarans, steady, slow, unfazed by any of the hurried activities.

The building could no longer hold up its own weight. It fell quickly, the structural support gone from underneath it. Everything cracked and crumbled. The second story area slid to the ground, covering the area where Drin had cut a hole.

He kept Anais's hand and dragged her after him. She jerked her hand away and ran with him once she realized what they were doing. The library rumbled and crashed. Another crumpled building in a city filled with destruction.

"Where are we going?" Anais asked.

"We should disappear into the forest, regroup with who we can. It's too dangerous in the city now. The Sekarans are all looking for us," Drin said.

"Follow me. There's a place I used to hide from my parents as a kid. It's hard to get to if you don't know where you're going, but it's safe," Anais said.

Drin allowed her to pass him so she could lead the way. He

hoped that would be the last he'd see of that battlemage, but he had a dreadful feeling it wouldn't be.

# TWENTY-EIGHT

ANAIS WAS TIRED OF RUNNING. IT SEEMED LIKE ALL SHE'D done since escaping Jafil's mansion involved fleeing from one place to another. Even though her legs didn't grow weary—both from her Pyus physiology primed to the task and because of the nanites' work keeping her energized—she couldn't help but feel they were on the losing end of the battle.

Everywhere they turned, waves of Sekaran soldiers flooded into the area, forcing them to take alternate routes into the forest. Once in the trees, in the darkness, Anais and Drin could obscure themselves well enough to evade battle, but they couldn't risk slowing down. She knew the way well enough that she could have made it to her childhood hiding spot with her eyes closed. But there was no joy in running there as there had been in years past. Just painful thoughts about the devastation leveled upon her world.

The night sky was filled with smoke. Some craft still flew around, Sekarans, hunting down the last of the mercenary ships in the area. Even though Anais had won almost every battle she'd been in with Drin, it felt like they were losing too much ground.

Shouldn't the occupation have ended when her old home was bombed? She hadn't heard from or seen the governor since then.

He was irrelevant now. Whoever commanded the current crop of Sekarans had his wits and fighting ability. This leader understood the flow of the battle, how to make gains. The Pyus who rose up to help her and the mercenaries would be hard-pressed to step up and fight again after they saw the results.

It made her hot with anger. She couldn't give up on her world. This was her home! And yet when the ships had started firing on the city, she'd abandoned her friends. They'd been separated when she decided to run with Drin, not even sparing a thought for the others. Where were they now? Err-dio? Elaym? Lyssa? She couldn't presume any of them made it out alive. They didn't have the benefit of the nanites to protect them.

She and Drin arrived at her hideaway. There was a small pond in the area, deep enough to swim in but not containing any fish. She missed those days of coming here in the summer, jumping in, cooling off. She'd been so innocent then. Would she ever be able to reclaim any sense of normalcy? With the world she'd been thrust into, probably not. But she couldn't live regretting that.

She slowed her pace at the edge of the water. The smoke in the air prevented the moonlight from shining on the pond. But she could see the area clearly through her nanite-aided vision. She turned to Drin. "Now what?"

Drin had his helmet on, but she could almost feel his stoic, frowning face behind it. He stayed steady like a rock throughout all of this. "Now we pray for guidance."

Anais opened her mouth to argue, but it wouldn't do any good. It was her failing, rushing into everything, and when he said things like this, it just highlighted where she needed to change. She hated it, but hated being wrong more. "Okay," she said.

Drin took her hands into his. A tingling sensation rushed through her. Even though his touch didn't signify what she desired, she loved having it. She tried to keep her mind off those things. "Yezuah, Lord, hear our prayer. You spoke to your followers and told them where two or more were gathered, you would be with us. We come to you now in humility, understanding we are flawed beings. Forgive us our sins. Make us clean and pure so we can have clarity as to the path you choose for us. Help us to smite your enemies and show us the path to saving the Pyus people," Drin said.

He let silence hang in the air for a long time, holding her hands. Anais grew anxious but didn't move. She stayed still, trying to focus on God. *Yes, please. We need your help.*

Rustling came from the bushes behind her, and Drin released her hands, forming his light sword faster than Anais could turn to see what was going on.

"Hold your fire!" said Raydon, the mercenary commander. He had his hands up, laser-repeater slung around his shoulder. A group of other mercenaries followed him. They carried wounded men with them. Elaym and Err-dio came up at the end of the pack.

"Elaym!" Anais ran forward and flung her arms around her old friend. She hadn't been sure whether he made it or not, and it was such a relief to see him. Tears streaked down her face. "I thought I'd lost you."

"Not yet, but it was close a couple of times," Elaym said. "It's madness out there."

"I know," Anais said, drawing back so she could see him. "I'm sorry we got separated."

"Me too."

"Have you seen Lyssa and the others?"

Elaym shook his head and then motioned to Err-dio. "Your six-armed friend here told me they split into two groups, people who wanted to help and resist, and others to protect for when the fighting was over. I'm not sure where the second group went."

Anais bit her lip. She hoped her friend was safe. After all they'd been through together, it would be awful to lose her.

"I'm sure they're safe. They'll be in one of the underground bunkers," Elaym said.

The mercenaries set down their wounded, using their packs as pillows to try to keep them comfortable. There were three men with terrible laser-repeater wounds. Bleeding, burns—they wouldn't last long. But Anais could change that.

She stepped from Elaym and crouched by the injured mercenaries. Healing was becoming a rote task for her now, something she could conjure through her nanites with no problems. She laid her hands on the first mercenary's wounds, letting the nanites go to work. Once they were done, she moved to the second and then to the third. It was the first time she'd done so many in a row without a breather, but she didn't want to risk their conditions worsening while they waited for herself to recover to full strength.

A dizzying sensation came over her, much like the first time she'd utilized her nanites to heal. The spinning became overwhelming, and Anais fell back on her rear. "I'm tired," she announced, as if it would do any good.

Raydon inspected his men's wounds, noting where they had been. "This is incredible. How did you do this?"

"Faith," Anais said.

Even though Drin was a few feet away, she could feel the nanites within her reacting with his. He projected a sense of pride for her. Go figure.

"Huh," Raydon said. "They're completely healed. It's like a miracle."

"Something to pay attention to," Drin said. "Through faith, all things are possible. I haven't wanted to preach to you, but it's my duty to remind you."

"I'll think about it," Raydon said. He looked up to the stars. The dark of night covered everything, making it impossible to see much. Only a couple of ships loomed in the atmosphere. Everything was peaceful, but the peace came because the Sekarans had pushed their small resistance back.

"What do we do next?" Anais asked, glancing back at Drin.

Drin crossed his arms. "We should probably rest until morning. There's nothing we can do now, and we need to ascertain the size of the current Sekaran force before making any decisions." He turned to Raydon. "Have you had any contact with your fleet?"

Raydon shook his head. "They haven't been answering. We took out the scattering field, but they might be engaged above, or..."

His words hung unfinished. What if Domen's ship and the other mercenary capital ships had been destroyed? It was a possibility. They'd be at the mercy of whatever forces the Sekarans had here. They were so close to freeing her people...but further than ever. "We have to do something. The Sekarans will redouble their efforts to harm my people."

"I wish there were a way to contact mine," Drin said, staring up at the stars.

Raydon produced his datapad again, tapping in commands. He waited for several moments. Lines formed around his eyes, betraying his age. "Still nothing," he said.

Drin shook his head. "We need something to break..."

More rustling came through the bushes. This time, the mercenaries scrambled to their feet, their rifles at the ready.

Unfortunately, even being ready, their movements were too little. Sekarans came out of the forest and into sight from every side. They were surrounded.

Worse, a battlemage pushed through the ranks of the Sekarans. The hard face was one Anais recognized as the one they had faced in the library earlier. He'd survived. His blood red eyes focused on them, face dripping with anger.

One of the mercenaries opened fire on the Sekarans, unable to hold his trigger. He shot one of the soldiers in the chest. The

Sekaran stumbled backward into his companions, falling to his death.

The Sekarans all returned fire at the mercenary. The whole unit lit him up in laser fire. The mercenary convulsed repeatedly, smoke rising from his body.

"Leo!" Raydon shouted, watching his companion fall to his death.

Then all hell broke loose.

# TWENTY-NINE

LASER FIRE ERUPTED EVERYWHERE. MOST OF THE mercenaries had the wherewithal to hit the ground. The ones slow to move received the brunt of the blasts.

Drin formed his light sword and rushed forward so he wouldn't get caught in too much of the crossfire. He had one target: the battlemage.

The bald, beady-eyed Sekaran formed a ball of energy in his hand and blasted it toward Drin. The energy slammed into his nanite shielding, causing it to flicker for the briefest of moments. Drin could absorb a few of those blasts, but it would get ugly quickly if he took too many of them straight on.

As he drew closer to the battlemage, the Sekaran reached to his belt to where there was a physical hilt. He drew it and produced his own light sword. "Shall we settle this in the old ways, Elorian?" the battlemage asked in a hissing tone.

"What about all of the soldiers firing on me? This is no duel," Drin said. He tested the battlemage with a quick jab of his light sword, but the battlemage deflected with his blade.

"Them? They are but flies to us, mere annoyances. You know

they're irrelevant. We are the true powers here." The battlemage laughed.

Something about his laugh unsettled Drin, but he was well aware the Sekaran meant to intimidate him, to cause him to lose focus. He wouldn't fall for those tricks. He'd had too much experience in battle. Instead, Drin feinted to try to draw the battlemage forward.

The trick worked. The battlemage thought he saw an opening, jabbing his light sword toward Drin's side, which he perceived as a mistake.

Drin turned to the side and landed a blow on the battlemage's arm. Smoke sizzled into the air where it hit.

The battlemage merely laughed again. "You're a serious one, aren't you? It will be quite fun severing your head when we're through with this game."

Giving Drin no time to react, he pushed forward. His blows came quickly, and Drin was barely able to keep up in parrying them. The battlemage moved with inhuman speed, swinging left and right and creating a near whirlwind with his blade. He left no openings. It forced Drin backward, into the middle of the crossfire of the main battle. Sekaran laser bolts slammed into his shielding. As much as the battlemage had said the others were mere annoyances, too many hits would be as deadly as the man standing in front of him. He needed support, but the mercenaries were too busy trying to recover and survive the initial ambush. They weren't faring well, judging from the bodies on the ground Drin had to be careful not to stumble over.

A ship flew overhead, creating a sonic boom as it passed. Weapons fire erupted in the sky, lighting up the battleground as if persistent lightning struck over and over again. Drin wanted to get a look at what was happening, but he couldn't risk giving the battlemage any opening.

One of the battlemage's thrusts succeeded in passing Drin's

defense, striking him in the arm in the same place the battlemage had been hit a few moments earlier. Drin gritted his teeth. The slice of laser energy burned. His whole arm flared up in pain.

The battlemage backed up to survey his handiwork, swinging his blade in a loop to his side. More intimidation tactics. "I believe the score is one to one. Do you wish to make a wager now? No? Probably best, since there won't be a way for me to collect from you when you're dead."

The respite in the action proved brief as he charged Drin again, this time with a strong blow downward and to the right, a move that very well could have severed Drin's neck.

Drin blocked this one and used the entirety of his strength to push the battlemage's light blade back.

"Oh my. Is that all you have? Are you tiring *already*? This is going to be far less fun than I thought." He cackled.

A loud explosion sounded above them. The noise was followed by the screeching sound of a crashing ship. The battlemage looked up, giving Drin an opening.

Drin drove his blade straight forward into the battlemage's side. It pierced him just below the ribs, but the battlemage recovered before the cut went too deep.

An expression of intense pain shot over the battlemage's face. Rage filled his eyes. "You're pestering me far too much, Elorian. It's not fun anymore." The wound sealed, battlemage magic preventing him from bleeding out. He redoubled his attacks on Drin, pushing harder than before.

Drin kept giving more and more ground. He backed into the middle of the battle. Laser bolts flew everywhere. The battlemage's relentless attacks began to wear Drin down. He couldn't keep up the fight at this pace for much longer. The Sekaran's angry stare turned into a wicked grin. He was enjoying every moment of breaking Drin.

The battlemage delivered another blow. Drin held his blade

up crosswise to block it. The battlemage took one of his hands off the hilt and formed energy in his hand. It was a small bubble of the energy, but it was enough. He shot it at Drin, and the force of it caused Drin to stumble. He ran right into the body of a fallen mercenary, tripping and falling backward across it. He couldn't keep his grip on his light sword as he fell, and the energy blade dissipated in the air.

The battlemage burst forward, holding his sword up over his head. He placed his boot on Drin's chest to pin him down. "Do you wish to recant your heresy before you die, Elorian?"

"Never," Drin said. He quickly uttered a prayer. *Lord Yezuah, forgive my sins and my failing. Allow me to enter into your kingdom clean and in service to you. Thank you for instilling the life in me you so graciously gave me. I am not afraid.*

The battlemage swung downward. Drin closed his eyes. He heard the buzzing sound of the light sword descend by him, but nothing hurt. He opened his eyes again.

The blade had missed to the side. And the battlemage's eyes were wide, mouth agape. Someone stood behind him. A light blade was driven directly into the implant by his skull.

Anais.

The woman pulled out her sword with a grunt. She took heavy breaths. "Oh, my God, it worked," she said, sounding amazed.

The battlemage wobbled and fell atop Drin, convulsing.

Drin pushed the Sekaran off him and sat up. "You used the same tactic I did. Going for his implant while he was distracted," Drin said.

"I might be a slow learner, but I still manage," Anais said. She offered a hand up.

Drin took it. It might have been the nanites assisting her strength, but she was able to pull him to his feet. "Thank you," Drin said.

"No problem. The fighting moved into the trees. I guess the

mercenaries didn't like being shot at out in the open. They regrouped with some more of theirs, and the Sekarans followed. I'm not sure who's winning."

"Thank you for the assessment," Drin said.

More lasers sounded overhead, followed by several *booms*. Fighters blew to bits, lighting up the sky. Anais looked up. "Are our mercenary reinforcements here?"

Drin glanced upward. His visor assisted him to filter out the smoky haze all around him and to be able to zoom in on the fighters above. There was intense dogfighting going on in the sky. The Sekaran ships tangled with their enemies—long, thin, needle-like craft. Drin recognized those immediately. "Those aren't the mercenaries above. Those are Elorian ships. My people are here."

Drin tapped his comm unit. "Drin to the *Justicar*. Come in."

Several moments passed. In the upper atmosphere, a much larger ship descended. The battleship Drin had spent the last several years upon. His home. His family.

"Templar Drin?" a voice said through the comm. "It's Commander Shayne. You didn't think we were going to leave you all on your own on this heathen world, did you?"

Drin smiled. "Shayne. It's good to hear your voice. The ground situation is complicated. There are far too many Sekarans."

"We've got them spotted and are sending a squadron to help you now."

As he said the words, some of the Elorian fighters broke off. They dropped to the tops of the trees before flattening out and zooming across the forest tops. They struck below with pinpoint laser shots. Dozens of bolts hit the ground. The bolts crackled into the trees ahead of Drin. Even from a distance, he heard shouts and cries of pain. The Sekaran forces wouldn't know what hit them.

Drin reformed his light sword into his hand and pushed through in the direction of the shouting. "Come on," he told Anais. "We're not done yet."

Anais formed her own light sword as they moved through the battlefield together. When they reached the forest, they came upon a unit of Sekarans. They weren't prepared to face the might of the Templars. Drin struck first, catching them by surprise. Anais stayed out of his way, though she followed dutifully. With the *Justicar* here, it would only be a matter of time before they cleared this planet of the threat.

# THIRTY

Anais stood in front of what once was her home, now a crumpled heap of rubble. Part of her wished Err-dio and the others had been a little more careful in the way they'd bombed what became the governor's mansion. As the crews started to clear the wreckage away, they found the bodies of the governor, his son, and Dr. Metayin. Anais couldn't help but feel a little heartache for the boy. She healed him, only for him to lose his life so soon afterward. It seemed like such a waste.

But it was better this way. With the governor dead, the Sekarans had very little ability to maintain their chokehold on the Pyus population. It had allowed for the Elorians to come in and finish off the Sekaran soldiers in the city. Though it would be months before things were back to normal on Pyus, reconstruction was already well underway. The transformer at the power station had been restored, allowing the street and traffic lights to function again. It also gave them access to Pyus's manufacturing facilities, so they could get supplies to those who needed it, and rebuild so many of the buildings that had been destroyed by the Sekaran threat.

Lyssa directed several of the workers, signing their work orders for the refuse removal. The team went to tear out the broken doors and glass away from the entrance. Lyssa stepped back toward Anais with her hands on her hips. "Good news. They think the blast didn't harm much of the structural integrity of your old home. The front area has pretty much been blown to pieces, but we can repair it, and we won't have to demolish the whole residence. You can even move back in if you don't mind occupying the western wing," she said.

"Since when did you get so good at managing projects?" Anais asked.

Lyssa shrugged. "Since I had to, I guess. Elaym is working on creating a new charter of merchant lords. The three of us are all that remain of the old families, so we'll be at the top of the new government when everything gets back to normal."

Anais nodded, but her heart wasn't overjoyed to hear the news. She'd held out some hope that some of her family had survived the Sekaran onslaught. Her father, mother, sisters, brothers...all gone. Did she even want to do the work of the merchant lords without them? She couldn't be so sure.

"I'm sorry," Lyssa said.

Anais turned to her and gave her a hug. "I'm sorry for you, too. It's so easy to wallow in our own pain. I don't want to forget you."

"I know you won't. You're the best friend anyone can ask for," Lyssa said.

Several Elorians appeared further down the street, walking toward them. It was a group of Templars, along with a couple of nuns, and a robed man Anais recognized as Father Cline. Drin walked by his side, and it looked like they were in serious discussion.

"Ah, Sister Anais, it's good to see you. I wanted to talk to both you and Drin together," Father Cline said. He motioned for the others to continue on. They did so without missing a step.

"Give us a moment, Lyssa?" Anais asked.

Lyssa nodded and returned to the construction crew.

Father Cline folded his hands in front of him. Drin stayed quiet. It was odd seeing him so deferential to someone else. Anais knew the Templars held Father Cline as their leader, but she imagined Drin's fighting spirit would overcome it. Instead, he fell into line.

"Thank you for indulging me," Father Cline said. "We found the Sekaran battleship and obliterated it. There will be no more raids on the city. Some of the Sekaran units fled into the deep forests, but our people are tracking them down and will finish them so they don't bother your people anymore."

Anais nodded. She was glad her world had been freed of the Sekarans, even if it had cost her a lot personally. Still, the victory didn't *feel* real. She was more worn out than anything else. Shouldn't winning feel more...like winning?

"But what I wanted to talk to the both of you about is your place in the Church. We are one body, the bride of Yezuah, here to maintain his household." He motioned all around them. "That is our divine purpose. The sword of righteousness and the amulet of healing are nothing if they are not attached to the body, do you understand?"

"Yes, Father," Drin said.

Anais nodded slightly, though she wasn't sure what he meant.

"Drin, you succeeded in liberating the world of Konsin on your own, but you are meant to be a part of the whole, with us in fraternity and unity. The reason the Church is here is for our togetherness, so we can operate as one in His divine purpose. I allowed you and Jellal to come to this world and help these people to show you you're not meant to go it alone. It was a lesson that cost you the life of your brother. But you need to understand patience, operating *with* the church, not apart from us."

"Does that mean you always intended on coming and helping

us?" Anais asked.

Father Cline nodded. "I had to obtain the approval of the bishops and cardinals, of course, which is why I needed time. But you should have waited and had patience. I, with my God-given wisdom, understood that if I told this to you at the time, you were likely to disobey and go anyway. These are your people, after all. I didn't want to put you in that position."

"Thank you, Father," Drin said.

Anais clutched the hem of her blouse. She was angry. He was intending on coming the whole time, and yet let them think they were stranded? For some lesson? It didn't seem right, nor fair. People died because of this.

Father Cline frowned at her. "I see you're angry, child. But you shouldn't be. You'll grow to understand in time. Drin needed to learn this lesson because there are many bigger battles to come. Trillions of lives could be at stake."

"We are approaching the final battle then?" Drin said.

"I believe we will see it within our lifetimes," Father Cline said.

The Final Battle? Anais didn't understand. She knew it had something to do with their religion—*her* religion—but she hadn't studied enough of their lore to have any clue as to what they were talking about.

"For now, our scouts have determined the Sekarans have built a new superweapon. This weapon can tear apart whole planets. They're constructing it now, deep within their territory. If they're able to get it online, we could lose everything."

"Point my blade and I shall deliver the vengeance of the Lord," Drin said.

Father Cline chuckled. "I'm sure you will. But you'll have to wait. We're still gathering the tactical data on the Sekaran world. We don't want to rush in." The words were a poignant reminder of what they'd done here. "For now, Templar Drin, I want you to train Sister Anais for the coming battles ahead, and your squire

Err-dio. So they might be more prepared. Do you think you can handle this task?"

"I do," Drin said.

Anais wanted to argue. She wasn't so sure she would be going with them into any battle. She still had her world here, a world in which she would be one of the top officials. Her people needed her as much as the Elorians did. Didn't they?

"You both have much to think on," Father Cline said. He reached out and squeezed both her and Drin's shoulders. "You are a blessing upon this universe. Never forget that." With those words, he nodded and turned to join the others.

Drin stood for a long moment in contemplation, then turned to Anais. "I was expecting punishment."

"You were? For what?" Anais asked.

Drin shrugged. "Never mind. Shall we get to training?"

"Now?" Anais asked. They had so much to do between reconstruction and getting the spaceport open for trade again.

"You'll need to master the nanites whether you stay here and help your people rebuild, or whether you come with us. Right now, you're on the right track, but you don't have instantaneous command of them as I do. I'll teach you to empty your thoughts, focus on God."

He understood her. Perhaps it was from the time their nanite fields interacted with each other. He was just more in tune with her than anyone else had ever been. It brought her joy to know he didn't judge her for not knowing what she wanted to do with her life. There would be merits to staying here and to going with them. But she couldn't just abandon her friends. At least she didn't have to make the decision today. Anais smiled at Drin, content she could spend more time with him. "Okay. Show me the way."

<<<<>>>>

# EXCERPT FROM GLORIFIED

Find out what happens next with Drin and Anais in the third book in the Saga of the Nano Templar, Glorified!

## Glorified

Drin parried the attack with little effort. His opponent chopped down at him with her light sword in a haphazard motion, easy to defend against. If Drin wished it, he could have delivered a kick to his opponent's torso, thrown her off guard, and stabbed her through the eye without breaking a sweat.

To an outsider, the sparks flying off the two energy weapons meeting would have appeared to be an impressive sight. The orange light reflected on the woman's furred face, her eyes tense with concentration, her lips pressed together. They had both formed their nanites into loose-fitting practice attire, having no need to don full battle armor.

In an ordinary battle, he would have sliced her into bits before she readied herself for her next blow. She wasn't ready for someone of his caliber. For now, he stayed on defense, allowing the woman to get a feel for the blade. She lacked the advantage of having been trained since being a young child with weapon in hand. Some people had to learn late. Drin could only hope it wasn't too late for her.

"Good," Drin said, despite thinking her form was anything but. She'd made improvements over the last time, which was the important part. "Watch your footwork. Keep yourself balanced so you can move fluidly."

"It's like dancing," said Anais, the woman across from him. She had long, floppy ears, which drooped over the sides of her head. She sweat through her white fur, causing her gray attire to cling to her lithe body.

It was distracting, but Drin tried to keep his focus away from her form. He had his vows of celibacy to consider, and Anais already tempted him far too much without his own stray thoughts aiding the effort. He pushed forward with his light sword, causing her to stumble backward. "Remember, when the two blades meet, you can use your body weight as if you were pushing on another object. Many swordsmen forget this with light swords, which you can use to your advantage."

Anais frowned, narrowing her eyes on him. "I don't think I'll ever be as good as you."

"Perhaps not, but Lord willing, you'll be able to hold your own."

She unleashed a flurry of blows on him, moving at a much more rapid pace than he could manage. Deklyn were faster than the Elorians as a whole. If she were a normal member of her species, Drin might have been able to match or even exceed her speeds with the help of the nanites, but she also had the advantage of the same ancient nanotechnology, which made the Templars the most notorious fighting force in the galaxy. Her speed made up for her inexperience and lesser strength.

Even with her rapid assault, Drin parried her every attack. He could see Anais was getting frustrated from an inability to pierce his defenses. She hadn't struck a single blow which penetrated to the shielding his nanites provided. The way her face tightened into impatience amused him. It reminded him of when he had to spar with his instructors as a teenager. He laughed.

"It's not..." Anais delivered her hardest strike to him yet, "...funny!"

"I'm sorry," Drin said. "Your face. If you could only see it..." He blocked the attack and pushed, forcing her off balance again. He thrust forward, a strike that if he had intended on hitting her would have killed her, but he intentionally let his blade slip to her side and past her. "Don't get angry during a fight. If you do, you'll allow your opponent an advantage. You need to keep your focus and calm."

"It's not as easy as it sounds," Anais spat back at him. She took in several deep breaths, circling him as she regained her composure.

She moved with the speed of the wind. Drin hadn't been ready for her to recover so quickly. Her movements were so rapid he couldn't draw his sword back in time to block this time. She struck to his side, causing his nanite field to react and capture the energy. It created a flickering pink glow around him.

Though the nanite field absorbed the shock, it couldn't completely dissipate the weapon's attack. It felt as if a wooden practice sword whacked him hard in the side, causing him to wince and stumble away from Anais's light sword.

"My God, are you okay?" Anais asked. She let her weapon dissipate, and she rushed to him, touching his off-hand arm gently. In the middle of a battle, it would have been a foolish move, though Anais didn't show the penchant for sustained combat. She empathized too much with other beings' pain. A noble trait, but one which would get her killed if she faced Sekarans with such a naive outlook.

Drin had to teach her a lesson.

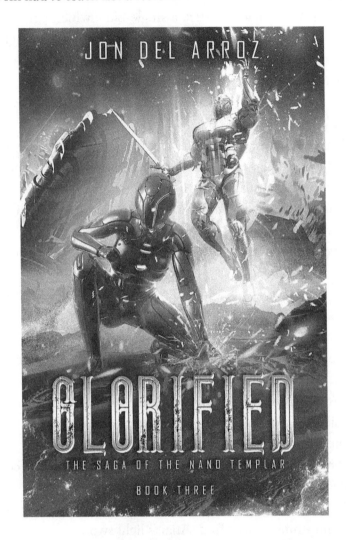

**A devastating superweapon...in the hands of galactic tyrants.**

The Sekaran fleet is gathering, asnd they've got a weapon that can destroy worlds.

Drin and his Templar brothers on the Justicar must face their deadliest battles yet, as the entire Elorian fleet is called into action to meet this threat.

But more than one planet killer awaits them. Deadly secrets from ancient races are hidden amongst the stars, and Drin must uncover the power of the mysteries of faith before it's too late.

Fans of Richard Fox's Terran Armor Corps and J.N. Chaney's Ruins Of The Galaxy will be enthralled by the epic conclusion to this military sci-fi trilogy. Purchase today!

# REVIEW REQUEST

Did you enjoy the book?

Why not tell others about it? The best way to help an author and to spread word about books you love is to leave a review.

If you enjoyed reading SANCTIFIED, can you please leave a review on Amazon for it? Good, bad, or mediocre, we want to hear from *you*. Jon and all of us at Silver Empire would greatly appreciate it.

Thank you!

# ABOUT JON DEL ARROZ

Jon Del Arroz is a #1 Amazon Bestselling author, "the leading Hispanic voice in science fiction" according to PJMedia.com, and winner of the 2018 CLFA Book Of The Year Award. As a contributor to The Federalist, he is also recognized as a popular journalist and cultural commentator. Del Arroz writes science fiction, steampunk, and comic books, and can be found most weekends in section 127 of the Oakland Coliseum cheering on the A's.

Keep up with Jon on his blog.

JOIN THE EMPIRE

# SILVER EMPIRE

Keep up with all the new releases, sneak peeks, appearances and more with the empire. Sign up for our Newsletter today!

Or join fellow readers in our Facebook Fan Group, the Silver Empire Legionnaires. Enjoy memes, fan discussions and more.

SANCTIFIED

SAGA OF THE NANO TEMPLAR, BOOK TWO

By Jon Del Arroz

Published by Silver Empire

https://silverempire.org/

 Created with Vellum

CPSIA information can be obtained
at www.ICGtesting.com
Printed in the USA
BVHW030215090621
609086BV00007B/198